Praise for Douglas Coupland

LIFE AFTER GOD
'Plainly, even beautifully written, in an achingly nostalgic
present tense'
The Times

'Compulsive'
Evening Standard

'A moving affirmation of secular spirituality'
Elle

SHAMPOO PLANET
'He accesses the prevailing culture, defines it and comments
on it . . . He has a powerhouse vocabulary and discerning
eye, plus as much empathy, sympathy and humanism as any
nineteenth century fiction hack filling readers in on the
Industrial Revolution. In time, he could generate as much
white noise as Don DeLillo'
Independent on Sunday

'You may shriek with laughter, you may weep manly tears
. . . Coupland's second novel is as dazzlingly disposable as his
Generation X . . . the author's philosophy is simple: pile up
enough one-liners and you get a novel. A very funny one'
Telegraph

'Captures the listlessness that accompanies growing up in
today's info-laden culture'
Rolling Stone

Life After God

Douglas Coupland

Scribner

First published in Great Britain by Simon & Schuster, 1994
This edition first published by Scribner, 1999
An imprint of Simon & Schuster UK Ltd
A Viacom Company

5 7 9 10 8 6 4

Simon & Schuster UK Ltd
Africa House
64-78 Kingsway
London WC2B 6AH

Simon & Schuster Australia
Sydney

A CIP catalogue record for this book is available from the British Library

ISBN 0-684-86021-X

Typeset by SX Composing DTP, Rayleigh, Essex
Cox & Wyman Ltd, Reading, Berkshire.

CONTENTS

LITTLE CREATURES

I was driving you up to Prince George to the home of your grandfather, the golf wino. I was tired – I shouldn't even have been driving such a long way, really – twelve hours of solid driving north from Vancouver. For the previous month, I had been living out of a suitcase and sleeping on a futon in a friend's den, consuming a diet of Kentucky Fried Chicken and angry recriminating phone calls with You-Know-Who. The nomadic lifestyle had taken its toll. I had been feeling permanently on the cusp of a flu, feeling at that point where I just wanted to borrow somebody else's coat – borrow somebody else's life – their aura. I seemed to have lost the ability to create any more aura on my own.

It was a jerky drive, punctuated by my having to stop at convenience stores and diners all along the way to try and reach my lawyer from pay phones. On the good side, however, *you* were noticing all of the animals in the world for the first time in your life – all of the animal life outside the car's windows. It started near the trip's beginning, in the farm lands of the Fraser Valley with its cows and sheep and horses. It became obsessive a half-hour later just past Chilliwack near the end of the valley when I pointed out a bald eagle sitting like a big stack of money beside the road atop a snaggy pine tree. You were so excited that you didn't even notice that the Flintstone Bedrock City amusement park was closed.

You asked questions about the animals, some real toughies, and these questions came as a welcome diversion from pay phones and tiredness. Just after you saw the eagle you asked me, seemingly out of the blue, *"Where do people come from?"* I wasn't sure if you meant the birds and bees or if you meant the ark or what have you. Either direction was a tad too much for me to handle just then, but you did get me to thinking. I mean, five thousand years ago people emerge out of nowhere – *sproing!* – with brains and everything and begin wrecking the planet. You'd think we'd give the issue more thought than we do.

You repeated your question again and so I gave you a makeshift answer of the sort parents aren't supposed to give. I told you people came "from back east." This seemed to satisfy you. And then at that point we both became distracted – you, by a blotch of racoon-based road kill that riveted your attention just off the highway's shoulder and me by another phone booth.

LIFE AFTER GOD

Lawyers – Jesus. Some day you cross this thin line and you really realize that we need to protect ourselves from ourselves.

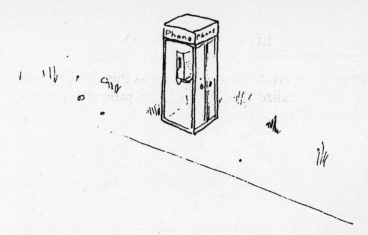

The phone call was long and filled with not-very-good news interrupted by 18-wheelers roaring past and by me yelling out at you not to poke the poor ex-racoon with a stick. I told Wayne, my lawyer, about the eagle, and he loved it, because he always calls his ego his eagle. "My eagle is soaring today." That kind of thing.

After slamming down the receiver I bought coffee and a 7-Up from the adjacent truck stop and we continued our drive, with you continuing your outlook for more animals, specifically bears and deer, as the valley turned into mountains. We turned on to the Coquihalla Highway and civilization melted away and I was relieved at how quickly the landscape became wild.

There was a dusting of snow on the upper reaches of the mountains, and there was a fresh smell coming through the vents, like Christmas trees. The end-of-day sunlight was strobing through the treetops beside us and in a valley below we saw a tuft of white birch that looked like the garnish on a Japanese meal. The road was so long and so steep, and the mountains so large, that I began to think of how the new world must have frightened and enchanted the pioneers. Our drive became serene.

I thought some more about the animals.

And this in turn made me think about humans. To be specific, I wondered about what it is that makes humans, well . . . *human?* What *is* human behavior? For example, we know what dog behavior is: dogs do doggy things – they chase sticks, they sniff bums and they stick their heads out of moving car windows. And we know what cat behavior is: cats chase mice, they rub up against your shin when they're hungry and they have trouble deciding whether or not they want to exit a door or stay inside when you go to let them out. So what exactly is it that *humans* do that is specifically human?

I looked at it a different way. I thought: here it is, as a species we've built satellites and cablevision and Ford Mustangs but what if, say, it was *dogs* and not people who had invented these things. How would *dogs* express their essential dogginess with inventions? Would they build space stations shaped like big bones that orbited the earth? Would they make movies of the moon and sit in drive-ins howling at the show?

Or what if it was *cats* and not humans who invented technology – would *cats* build scratching-post skyscrapers covered entirely with shag carpeting? Would they have TV shows starring rubber squeak toys?

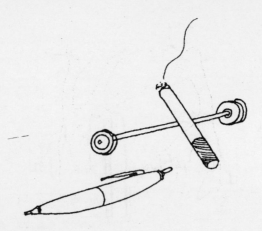

But it wasn't other animals who invented machines, it was *humans*. So what is it about our essential *humanity* that we are expressing with our inventions? What is it that makes us *us*?

I thought of how odd it is for billions of people to be alive, yet not one of them is really quite sure of what makes people *people*. The only activities I could think of that humans do that have no other animal equivalent were smoking, body-building, and writing. That's not much, considering how special we seem to think we are.

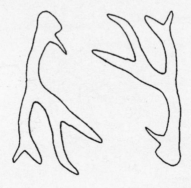

Below us on the right, the Coquihalla River raged. The car cruised along smoothly. Then, just after we emerged from the second of two snowsheds we saw some white-tailed deer – a stag, a doe and a knob-antlered yearling. You got overexcited, like you'd just had five bowls of Count Chocula. We stopped the car and got out to look and became deadly silent. The three creatures gave us only the most brief, innocently curious glance before delicately bounding back into their woods. Getting back into the car I said to you, "I wonder what animals must make of human beings with our crazy red cars and colorful clothing. What do you think, eh? They must think us people are the freakiest things going." You paid no attention to this.

Then we drove not even a mile further and we saw two bighorn sheep on a ridge, scrambling down a plume of gravel. Again we stopped the car and got out. Even though it was awfully cold, high up in the mountains, we watched these two creatures until they, too, vanished into their forest.

We drove away and we were both quiet, digesting the appearances of these animals in our lives, and their meanings. What is a deer? What is a bighorn sheep? Why are certain creatures attractive to some of us, and some not? What *are* creatures?

I thought of my own likes. I like dogs because they always stay in love with the same person. Your mother likes cats because they know what they want. I think that if cats were double the size they are now, they'd probably be illegal. But if dogs were even three times as big as they are now, they'd still be good friends. Go figure.

You like all animals at the moment, although no

doubt you will one day choose your favorites. Your own nature will triumph. We are all born with our natures. You popped out of your mother's belly, I saw your eyes, and I knew that you were already *you*. And I think back over my own life and I realize that my own nature – the core *me* – essentially hasn't changed over all these years. When I wake up in the morning, for those first few moments before I remember where I am or when I am, I still feel the same way I did when I woke up at the age of five. Sometimes I wonder if natures can be changed at all or if we are stuck with them as surely as a dog wants bones or as a cat chases mice.

We stopped for dinner in the town of Merritt at the Chicken Shack. You brought in some of your books to read while my red eyes scanned *The Globe and Mail* like a stick being scraped back and forth over the pavement.

Afterward we resumed our drive. The sky had a lavender glaze and the mists on the top of the mountain peaks were like a world that was still only at the idea stage. We cut into a fog in a valley, as though driving into the past.

We then crested a hill and descended into another valley, where a flock of unknown birds were floating down the center of a deep canyon, as though locked in amber. And then we descended into the canyon where there were no houses or sounds – just us and the road – and a snow began to fall and the sun began to fail completely and the world turned milky and I said, "Hold your breath" and you said, "Why?" and I said, "Because we're entering the beginning of time." And we did.

Time, Baby – so much, so much time left until the end of my life – sometimes I go crazy at how slowly time passes yet how quickly my body ages.

But I shouldn't allow myself to think like this. I have to remind myself that time only frightens me when I think of having to spend it alone. Sometimes I scare myself with how many of my thoughts revolve around making me feel better about sleeping alone in a room.

We stayed at a motel in Kamloops that night, halfway to our ultimate destination. I just couldn't make it any further. After we got settled into our room, the big drama was that we forgot your Dr. Seuss book back at the Chicken Shack in Merritt. You refused to settle down until I told you a story and so I was forced to improvise in spite of my tiredness, something I am not good at doing. And so out of nowhere, I just said what came into my head and I told you the story of "Doggles."

"Doggles?" you asked.

"Yes – Doggles – the dog who wore goggles."

And then you asked me what did Doggles *do*, and I couldn't think of anything else aside from the fact that he wore goggles.

You persisted and so I said to you, "Well, Doggles was supposed to have had a starring role in the *Cat in the Hat* series of books except . . ."

"Except what?" you asked.

"Except he had a drinking problem," I replied.

"Just like Grandpa," you said, pleased to be able to make a real life connection.

"I suppose so," I said.

So then you wanted to hear about another animal, and so I asked you if you'd ever heard of Squirrelly the Squirrel, and you said you hadn't. So I said, "Well, Squirrelly was going to have an exhibition of nut paintings at the Vancouver Art Gallery except . . ."

"Except what?" you asked.

"Except Mrs. Squirrelly had baby squirrels and so Squirrelly had to get a job at the peanut butter factory and was never able to finish his work."

"Oh."

I paused. "You want to hear about my other animals?"

"Un, I guess so," you replied, a bit ambiguously.

"Did you ever hear of Clappy the Kitten?"

"No."

"Well, Clappy the Kitten was going to be a movie star one day. But then she rang up too many bills on her MasterCard and had to get a job as a teller at the Hongkong Bank of Canada to pay them off. Before long she was simply too old to try becoming a star – or her ambition disappeared – or both. And she found it was easier to just talk about doing it instead of actually doing it and . . ."

"And what," you asked.

"Nothing, baby," I said, stopping myself then and there – feeling suddenly more dreadful than you can imagine having told you about these animals – filling your head with these stories – stories of these beautiful little creatures who were all supposed to have been part of a fairy tale but who got lost along the way.

MY HOTEL YEAR

1 Cathy

It was years ago. I had been going through a patch of intense brooding and had made a big hubbub about severing most of my ties to my past. I had moved into a rent-by-the-week cold water downtown hotel room on Granville Street and had cut all my hair off, stopped shaving, and had thorns tattooed on my right arm. I spent my days lying on my bed staring at the ceiling, listening to the drunken brawls in other rooms, the squawk of other TVs and the smashing of other mirrors. My fellow tenants were a mixture of pensioners, runaways, drug dealers and so forth. The whole ensemble had made a suitably glamorous backdrop for my belief that my poverty, my fear of death, my sexual frustration and my inability to connect with others would carry me off into some sort of Epiphany. I had lots of love to give – it's just that no one was taking it then. I had thought I was finding consolation in solitude, but to be honest I think I was only acquiring a veneer of bitterness.

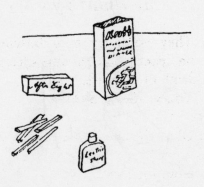

My neighbors across the hall at this time were a headbanger couple, Cathy and Pup-Tent. Cathy was a seventeen-year-old runaway from Kamloops up north; Pup-Tent was a bit older and from back East. They both had the ghostly complexions, big hair and black leather wardrobe that heavy metal people like so much. They tended to live at night and sleep late into the afternoon, but sometimes I would see Pup-Tent being the very picture of enterprise down on Granville Street, selling hashish cut with Tender Vittles to treeplanters on city leave. Or I would see Cathy, selling feather earrings in the rain on Robson Street. Sometimes I would see them both at the corner grocery store where they would be shopping for Kraft dinner, grenadine syrup, peeled carrot sticks, Cap'n Crunch, After Eight dinner mints and Lectric Shave. We would nod in a neighborly way and occasionally we would meet in the pub at the Yale Hotel where we would get to talking, and it was via these encounters that I got to know them. They would sit there drawing skulls and crossbones on each other's transdermal nicotine patches and drink draft beers.

Pup-Tent: You want to talk?

Cathy: No.

Pup-Tent: Okay then.

(A pause.)

Cathy: Stop ignoring me.

By themselves they could be interesting, but as a twosome their conversation was a bit limited. Sometimes it is nice to sit with people and not say much of anything.

But any adoration in their relationship was strictly one-way. Cathy was in love with Pup-Tent – her first love – whereas I suspect Pup-Tent saw Cathy as just an interchangeable girlfriend unit. He would "keep her in line" by flaunting the ease with which he could seduce other women. He was good looking by any standard, and his main pick-up technique was to pump out negative signals so that women with low self-esteem would be glued to him. In this way he could always have the upper hand. A not-so-fresh barfly would ask him, "How old do you think I am, cutie?" and Pup-Tent would reply, "Thirty-three and divorced – or twenty-eight with a drinking problem." If she was his type, then she'd be hooked then and there.

This flirting drove Cathy crazy. Sometimes when Pup-Tent disappeared from the table she would tell me so. When Cathy's sister, Donna, came down from Kamloops to visit one day and sat with us, she asked Cathy what it was she saw in Pup-Tent. "Let me get this straight, Cath: jail record . . . violent . . . no job . . ."

"Oh," Cathy replied, "but I like the way he *walks*."

On evenings when Pup-Tent and I were by ourselves at the pub, he would ask me things such as, "How come a woman screwed up on drugs is so much scarier than a guy screwed up on drugs?" And I would reply, "Is this a joke?" and he'd say, "No, I'm really asking you."

In general, though, they seemed affable enough with each other, and most of the time their conversation moved along predictable lines.

Pup-Tent: "Why are you staring at me?"

Cathy: "I'm wondering what you're thinking about."

Pup-Tent: "Why do you care what I think?"

Cathy: "Okay, I don't."

Pup-Tent: "Then prove it by minding your own business."

After a while, though, the two of them began having fights that were loud enough to wake me up from across the hall. Cathy would appear on the street with the occasional bruise or red eyeball. But as with most couples involved in this sort of relationship, the subject of domestic violence never came up in their conversations with others.

One day Cathy, myself and a street kid – a male exotic dancer on his day off – were discussing death over a plate of fries with gravy at Tat's Coffee Inn. The question was, "What do you think dying is like?" Cathy said it was like you're in a store and a friend drives up to the front door in a beautiful car and says "Hop in – let's go on a trip!" And so you go out for a spin. And once you're out on the road and having a great time, suddenly your friend turns to you and says, "Oh, by the way, you're dead," and you realize they're right, but it doesn't matter because you're happy and this is an adventure and this is fine.

Once, on a morning after a particularly noisy night, Cathy and I were walking down Drake Street and we saw a crow standing in a puddle, motionless, the sky reflected on its surface so that it looked as though the crow was standing on the sky. Cathy then told me that she thinks that there is a secret world just underneath the surface of our own world. She said that the secret world was more important than the one we live in. "Just imagine how surprised fish would be," she said, "if they knew all the action going on just on the other side of the water. Or just imagine yourself being able to breathe underwater and living with the fish. The secret world is that close and it's *that* different."

I said that the secret world reminded me of the world of sleep where time and gravity and things like that don't matter. She said that maybe they were both the same thing.

One day I came home from the library, where I had
spent the afternoon trying to make people feel
middle class by scowling at them. The door to Cathy
and Pup-Tent's apartment was wide open so I poked
my head in and said "Hello?" I couldn't believe what a
dump their place was – strewn with rusting bike
chains, yellowed house plants, cigarette boxes and
butts, Metallica banners, beer bottles, grubby blankets
and Cathy's clothes. I said, "Cath? Pup? You guys in?"
but there was no answer.

I stood there looking around when Cathy came in
the door looking in awful condition and carrying a bag
of Burger King food. She said that Pup-Tent was gone,
that he'd taken off with a stripper to Vancouver Island
and that, in the end, he had gone nuts because Cathy
had erased all of his cassette tapes by microwaving
them in his mini microwave.

"I must look pretty bad, huh?"

"No," I said, "not at all."

"You hungry? Want some food?"

"Maybe later."

We stood in silence for a little while. Cathy picked up a few stray garments. Then she said, "You used to live over on the mountain, didn't you – over on the North Shore?"

I confirmed I had grown up there.

"That's where the big lake is, right – the reservoir?"

I told her this was true.

"Then I need you to help me with something – what are you doing this afternoon?"

I replied what am I *ever* doing in the afternoons.

Cathy wanted to see the water reservoir up the Capilano Canyon, up behind Cleveland Dam. She wouldn't tell me why until we got there, but she seemed in an obviously unhappy state and playing tour guide was the least I could do to cheer her up. And so we took the bus over to the North Shore, to the mountains overlooking the city.

The bus climbed up Capilano Road, past the suburban houses nested inside the tall Douglas firs, hemlocks and cedars. These houses seemed far enough away from my present life as to seem like China.

Further up the mountain, the late-afternoon sky was cloudy and dark. When the wet air from the Pacific Ocean hits the mountains, it dumps all of its wetness right there. The sky was just starting to rain as we got off the bus near the Cleveland Dam and, as we crossed the road, I could tell we were going to get soaked.

The reservoir itself was a short walk away and was quickly enough pointed out to Cathy, but she looked disappointed when she saw it, though – the large, loch-like lake stretching back into the steep, dark mountain valley. She said, "like, what's with the barbed wire fence – you mean we can't go in and touch the water?"

I said we couldn't – not from where we were.

"We have another option?"

I said we did, but it would involve some tromping

through the woods and she said this was just fine, and so we headed up the road past a sign saying: WATERSHED: NO ADMITTANCE to a place where we used to have outdoor parties when I was in high school.

Cathy sullenly smoked a cigarette and clutched her purse to her side as we walked past a gate and up the dirt access road. The mountains above us were cloaked in mist up at their tops and we heard only the occasional bird noise as we cut off the road and into the trees. Cathy was immediately drenched as we cut through the underbrush of salmonberry bushes, grasses and juvenile firs. Her big hair was filled with spider-webs and fir needles and dead huckleberry leaves; her black jeans were wet and clammy at her ankles. I asked her if she wanted to go back but she said, no, we had to continue and so we did, tromping deep into the black echo-free woods until we saw the glint of water ahead of us – the reservoir. Cathy then said to me, "Stop – don't move," and I froze.

I thought she had seen a bear or had pulled a gun out of her purse. I turned around and she had frozen in mid-motion. She said, "I bet if we froze right here and didn't move and didn't breathe we could stop time."

And so we stood there, deep in the woods, frozen in mid-motion, trying to stop time.

Now: I believe that you've had most of your important memories by the time you're thirty. After that, memory becomes water overflowing into an already full cup. New experiences just don't register in the same way or with the same impact. I could be shooting heroin with the Princess of Wales, naked in a crashing jet, and the experience still couldn't compare to the time the cops chased us after we threw the Taylors' patio furniture into their pool in the eleventh grade. You know what I mean.

I think Cathy at some level also felt this way, too – and that she realized all of her important memories would be soon enough taken – that she had X-numbers of years ahead of her of falling for the wrong guys – mistreaters and abusers – and that all of her memory would then be used up in sadness and dead ends and being hurt, and at the end of it all there would be . . . nothing – no more new feelings.

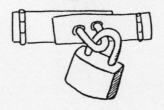

Sometimes I think the people to feel the saddest for are people who are unable to connect with the profound – people such as my boring brother-in-law, a hearty type so concerned with normality and fitting in that he eliminates any possibility of uniqueness for himself and his own personality. I wonder if some day, when he is older, he will wake up and the deeper part of him will realize that he has never allowed himself to truly exist, and he will cry with regret and shame and grief.

And then sometimes I think the people to feel saddest for are people who once knew what profoundness was, but who lost or became numb to the sensation of wonder – people who closed the doors that lead us into the secret world – or who had the doors closed for them by time and neglect and decisions made in times of weakness.

What happened was this: Cathy and I walked to the edge of the reservoir's water and from her purse she removed a Ziploc baggie containing two filmy-tailed, rather stupid-looking goldfish that Pup-Tent had bought for her the week before in an isolated moment of kindness. We sat down on the smooth rocks next to the spotless, clean, infinitely dark and deep lake water. She said to me, "You only get once chance to fall in love for the first time, don't you." And I said, "Well, at least you got the chance. A lot of people are still waiting."

She then poked into the glassy still water, made small ripples, and threw a stone or two. Then she took the baggie, placed it under the water and punctured the membrane with her sharp black fingernails. "Bye-bye, fishies," she said as the two languidly wriggled away down into the depths. "Make sure you two stay together. You're the only chance that either of you is ever going to get."

2 *Donny*

Donny was a hustler who lived at the end of the hall in the tiny room next to the bathroom. He was young and friendly, and sometimes would ask me to have dinner with him, but dinner usually turned out to be blue Popsicles, Velveeta cheese and beer in his dingy room where the paint peeled and you could see how many colors the room had been before. The only technology in the room was a phone and a phone answering machine he used to reply to ads he placed in the paper. I'd feel so sorry for him. Even though I was broke I'd find a way to treat him to dinner at the A&W.

Donny would do anything with anybody, but mostly people didn't want to do much, he said. A sixteen-year-old girl asked him to sit in a hot tub with her with no clothes; an older yuppie-type business-woman paid him $250.00 just to go see *Batman Returns* with her. Donny said it was things like this that really made him wonder about human nature – not the jobs where people wore leather masks and kicked him in the stomach.

Every afternoon around dark, when the windows got dark enough to turn into mirrors, Donny would come out of the bathroom with wet short black hair which he would shake like a dog, and then tramp down the hotel's creaky old stairs and pursue the evening's commerce. He said he thought of himself as an entrepreneur; he said the guys on the street gave him the nickname Puttáno, Boy Slut; he said anything was better than the job he had before, which involved driving a shuttle bus between the airport and one of the downtown hotels.

Oddly, Donny had an accountant, Meyer, a 12-step meeting addict from the first floor. Meyer made Donny take out ads saying "I will tell you my deepest fantasy . . . Mail $20.00 in a S.A.S.E. to STUD MAN, P.O. Box . . ." The ad was in case the tax people ever decided to get on Donny's case and he needed a way to launder his money. As if! I imagine any money Donny might have saved was to fund his idea for the future, which he mentioned once and only once. The idea was to "hook a whole bunch of suntanning beds up to a computer and have little girls pushing the buttons for me at $3.25 an hour."

Donny was always getting stabbed. His skin was beginning to look like an old leather couch at the Greyhound station, but this did not bother him at all. One night after a flare up on a sidewalk after an Alexis-versus-Krystle drag night at one of the clubs, Donny came home with a half dozen calligraphic red slashes all over his stomach. I tried to make him go to St. Paul's for stitches but he wouldn't. When I asked him if he was worried about permanent damage he gave me a guarded look and said, "This is my life and this is how I live it." I never hassled him again after that.

But Donny actively invited stabbing into his life. He said that stabbing didn't hurt nearly as much as you'd think and that it was actually kind of cool, and that when it happened, "man, when that blade first digs into you it makes your soul leap out of your body for just a second, like a salmon jumping out of a river."

I do remember him telling me, though, that he was actually getting a little bored of being stabbed. He said that in the end his big goal was to get shot. He was so curious to know what being shot would be like. To facilitate shooting he would always wear his shirts wide open at the chest, like a 1976 person.

Donny showed up nearer the end of my stay at the hotel – a period when I was wondering if I would eventually be exhausted by the effort it was taking to cope with solitude.

I think it takes an amazing amount of energy to convince oneself that the Forever Person isn't just around that next corner. In the end I believe we never do convince ourselves. I know that I found it increasingly hard to maintain the pose of emotional self-sufficiency lying on my bed and sitting at my desk, watching the gulls cartwheeling in the clouds over the bridges, cradling myself in my own arms, breathing warm chocolate-and-vodka breath on a rose I had found on a street corner, trying to force it to bloom.

Time ticks by; we grow older. Before we know it, too much time has passed and we've missed the chance to have had other people hurt us. To a younger me this sounded like luck; to an older me this sounds like a quiet tragedy.

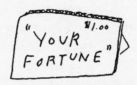

Sometimes Donny and Cathy and me would walk the streets together on a sunny day and just bum around. The innocence of this activity made our lives seem a bit less dark. We would buy ice creams, Donny would walk on his hands and we would play "mock the stock" at some of the more extreme bondage and sex stores.

Once in the early evening we walked past a fortune teller – a grizzled old soak sitting forlornly behind a card table clutching a deck of tarot cards probably salvaged from a dumpster and a Japanese paper carp with a candle burning inside. We kidded Donny and said he should have his fortune read, but he freaked and refused flat out. "I'm not having some old rubby tell me my future. Man, he probably lives in an old fridge under the Burrard Bridge. He probably sits in his fridge and molests tennis starlets all day."

We didn't press the issue, and if the fortune teller had heard Donny's comments, he gave no indication and we walked on.

It was only a few weeks later that I saw Donny, cheerfully being told his fortune by the same old fortune teller. I walked up to him and said, "Hey, Sport – I thought you didn't want to have your fortune told to you."

And Donny said matter-of-factly, "Hey, guy. Didn't you see the sign here?" He pointed to some words lopsidedly felt-penned on a sheet of packing cardboard next to the candle which read:

I PROMiSS I wonT TeLL YOu YOuR gOING TO DIE.

"That's all it takes, Man. It's all I ever wanted to hear. Keep on reading, Mister."

This is not a long story. In the end Donny got his wish and he did get shot – over a very stupid drug deal that imploded in a Chinatown parking lot – twice in the back of the head and once in the back. I ended up having to identify the body as nobody knew where his family was or who they were. I guess his salmon jumped out of the river and on to land and the river itself flows on.

I left the hotel shortly thereafter and, very soon after that, I fell in love. Love was frightening and it hurt – not only during, but afterward – when I fell out of love. But that is another story.

I would like to fall in love again but my only hope is that love doesn't happen to me so often after this. I don't want to get so used to falling in love that I get curious to experience something more extreme – whatever that may be.

THINGS THAT FLY

For anyone who's ever
broken up with someone else

I'm sitting hunched over the living room coffee table on a Sunday night, in a daze, having just woken up from a deep deep sleep on a couch shared with pizza boxes and crushed plastic cherry yogurt containers. In front of me a TV game show is playing on MUTE and my head rests on top of my hands, as though I am praying, but I am not; I am rubbing my eyes and trying to wake up, and my hair is brushing the tabletop which is covered in crumbs and I am thinking to myself that, in spite of everything that has happened in my life, I have never lost the sensation of always being on the brink of some magic revelation – that *if only* I would look closely enough at the world, then that magic revelation would be mine – *if only* I could wake up just that little bit more, then . . . well – let me describe what happened today.

Today went like this: I was up at noon; instant coffee; watched a talk show; a game show; a bit of football; a religious something-or-other; then I turned the TV off. I drifted listlessly about the house, from silent room to silent room, spinning the wheels of the two mountain bikes on their racks in the hallway and straightening a pile of CDs glued together with spilled Orange Crush in the living room. I suppose I was trying to pretend I had real things to do, but, well, I didn't.

My brains felt overheated. So much has happened in my life recently. And after hours of this pointlessness I finally had to admit I couldn't take being alone one more moment. And so I swallowed my pride and drove to my parents at their house further up the hill here on the North Shore: up on the mountain – up in the trees to my old house – my true home, I guess. Today was the first day when I could really tell that summer was over. The cold air sparkled and the maple leaves were rotting, putting forth their lovely reek, like dead pancakes.

Up on the mountain, my mother was in the kitchen making 1947-style cream cheese sandwiches with pimentos and no crusts to freeze in advance for her bridge friends. Dad was sitting at the kitchen table reading *The Vancouver Sun*. Of course they knew about what had happened recently and so they were walking on eggshells around me. This made me feel odd and under-the-microscope, so I went upstairs to sit in the guest room to look out the window at honking V's of Canada geese flying south toward the United States from northern British Columbia. It was peaceful to see so many birds flying – to see all these things in our world that can fly.

Mom had left the TV on in the bedroom, next room over. CNN was saying that Superman was scheduled to die later this week – in the sky above Minneapolis, and I was momentarily taken out of myself. I thought this was certainly a coincidence, because I had just visited the city of Minneapolis a month ago, on a business trip: a new crystal city, all shiny like quartz rising over the Midwest corn fields. According to the TV, Superman was supposed to die in an air battle over the city with a supremely evil force, and while I knew this was just a cheesy publicity ploy to sell more comics – and I haven't even *read* a Superman comic in two decades – the thought still made me feel bad.

And then the geese passed, and I sat watching the blue smoke linger down the mountain slopes from people burning leaves across the Capilano River. After a while I returned downstairs and Dad and I sat in the kitchen next to the sliding glass door and we fed the birds and animals on the back patio. We had grain and corn for the chickadees, juncos and starlings; and roasted peanuts for the jays and the black and grey squirrels. Such a sea of life! And I was glad for this activity because there is something about the animals that takes us out of ourselves and takes us out of time and allows us to forget our own lives.

Dad had placed a cob of corn on a stump for the jays, who bickered over it non-stop. And we threw peanuts to the jays and I noticed that when I threw two peanuts to a jay, it just sat there and couldn't decide which nut was juicier, so it became paralyzed with greed and couldn't take either of them. And we threw nuts to the squirrels, too, and they're so dumb that even if I hit them on the head with a nut, they couldn't find it. I just don't know how they've managed to survive these millions of years. Dad had also scattered sunflower seeds for a flying squirrel he has named Yo-yo who lives in the backyard. Yo-yo darted about the yard like a pinball.

Mom said that people are interested in birds only inasmuch as they exhibit human behavior – greed and stupidity and anger – and by doing so they free us from the unique sorrow of being human. She thinks humans are tired of having to take the blame all by themselves for the badness in the world.

I told Mom my own theory of why we like birds – of how birds are a miracle because they prove to us there is a finer, simpler state of being which we may strive to attain.

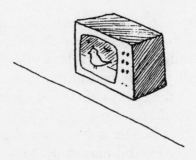

But anyway, I began feeling low again, and I felt I was making Mom and Dad feel uncomfortable because they were worrying I might go to pieces at any moment. I could see the relief on their faces when I laughed at the jays, like I'd been cured, and this depressed me, made me feel like a freak, and so I went back upstairs, into the TV room, turned on the TV and hid. I got to thinking about all of the bad stuff that had happened in life recently. It made me think of all of the bad things I had done to other people in my world – and there have been so many bad things I have done. I felt ashamed; I was feeling as though none of the good deeds I had ever done had ever mattered.

And on the TV there were still more birds! Such lovely creatures and I thought that we are so lucky to have the animals. What act of goodness did we as humans once commit to deserve such kindness from God?

There was a pretty grey parakeet who had learned to recognize human things – triangle shapes and car keys and the color blue – and to speak the words for them. This little parakeet worked so hard to remember these things, and it had an efficient faraway female voice like a telephone operator in Texas. The parakeet made me realize how hard it is to learn anything in life, and even then, there's no guarantee you might need it.

On another channel there were pictures of a zoo in Miami, Florida, which had been whacked by a hurricane and there were pictures of ducks and tall elegant birds swimming in the wreckage except they didn't know it was wreckage. It was just the world.

And then there was the same news story again about Superman's dying – except I realized I got the city wrong – he's supposed to die over *Metropolis*, not Minneapolis. But I was still sad. I have always liked the idea of Superman because I have always liked the idea that there is one person in the world who doesn't do bad things. And that there is one person in the world who is able to fly.

I myself often have dreams in which I am flying, but it's not flying the way Superman does. I simply put my arms behind my shoulders and float and move. Needless to say, it is my favorite dream.

Back on TV there were pictures of whooping cranes doing a mating dance and they were so sweet and graceful and I thought "If only *I* could be a whooping crane and was able to float and fly like them, then it would be like always being in love."

And then I got just plain lonely and just so fed up with all the badness in my life and in the world and I said to myself, "Please, God, just make me a bird – that's all I ever really wanted – a white graceful bird free of shame and taint and fear of loneliness, and give me other white birds among which to fly, and give me a sky so big and wide that if I never wanted to land, I would never have to."

But instead God gave me these words, and I speak them here.

And I will add in closing that when I got back home tonight, I stepped through the door and over my messes; I fell on to the couch and into a sleep and then into a dream, and I dreamed that I was back in Minneapolis, back next to the corn fields. I dreamed I had taken a glass elevator to the top of one of the city's green glass skyscrapers, to the very top floor, and I was running around that floor from one face of the skyscraper to another, frantic, looking through those big sheets of glass – trying to find a way to protect Superman.

THE WRONG SUN

1 *Thinking of the Sun*

The first time I ever visited a McDonald's restaurant was on a rainy Saturday afternoon, November 6, 1971. It was Bruce Lemke's 10th birthday party, and the McDonald's was at the corner of Pemberton Avenue and Marine Drive in North Vancouver, British Columbia. The reason I can pinpoint this date is that it was also the date and time of the Cannikin nuclear test on Amchitka Island in the Aleutians – a Spartan Missile warhead of between 4 and 5 megatons was detonated at the bottom of a 1.5 mile vertical shaft drilled into this Alaskan island. The press had made an enormous to-do over this blast, as it was to be roughly four times more powerful than any previous under-ground detonation. According to the fears of the day, the blast was to occur on seismic faults connected to Vancouver, catalyzing chain reactions which in turn would trigger the great granddaddy of all earthquakes. The Park Royal shopping center would break in two and breathe fire; the Cleveland Dam up the Capilano

River would shatter, drowning whoever survived in the mall below. The cantilevered L-shaped modern houses with their "Kitchens of Tomorrow" perched on the slopes overlooking the city would crumble like so much litter – all to be washed away by a tsunami six hours later.

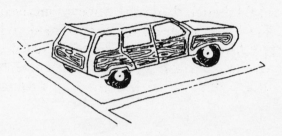

I remember sitting on my purple vinyl stool being unable to eat, gazing out the window, waiting for the flash, waiting for the cars to float up into the sky, for the Hamburglar statue to melt, for the tiled floor to break apart and expose lava.

Of course, nothing happened. A half hour later we were driving away in Mrs. Lemke's station wagon to see *The Railway Children* at the Park Royal Twin Theaters. But connections had been made in my mind, however – connections which are hard for me to sever even now, twenty years later: one, that McDonald's equals evil; two, that technology does not always equal progress.

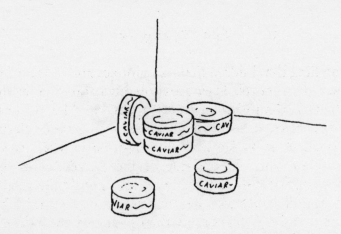

Another nuclear episode, a cherished family story. It is the night of October 20, 1962, and my mother is attending a dance in the officers' mess of the Canadian Air Force base at Baden-Söllingen, West Germany, my birthplace. I am 294 days old. My father is in Switzerland on air force business that evening. An aide-de-camp enters the dance and begins whispering into the ears of the jet fighter pilots. Within minutes, the pilots melt away from the dance, off to the runway where they are then strapped into their jets and placed on 24-hour shifts, and the women are left confused and standing by themselves in Dior "New Look" inspired dresses. They shuffle perplexedly back into the private married quarters – the PMQ's – where they pay the babysitters and search through their cupboards for supplies of powdered milk. The Zenith shortwave radio is turned on and is not turned off for the next three days.

The next day, the PX is closed. Mothers take shifts

watching the children in the sandboxes and monitoring the radio reports. They are probably calmer about the situation than civilian wives might be. Already base wives have been through other crises and alerts, though none as large as this. Europe in 1962 is an arena of fear. To the side of the Autobahn in the scrawny firs of the Schwarzwald lurk untold thousands of camouflaged tanks. Jets buzz the base every day. The Iron Curtain is never more than a tank of gas away.

The crisis builds. For the first time the women are escorted into the "bunkers" – unused furniture storage lockers with windows on the ground floors of the PMQs. There is no furniture inside, nor food nor supplies – no diapers, tranquilizers, bandages, or clean water. Oddly there *is*, though, six tins of caviar sitting in a corner. When the women complain they are told by base authorities that they are expendable. *"You should have known that before you came overseas with your husbands."*

The women sit in the semi-dark and monitor the radio while the babies cry. The women look up at the skies, wondering what comes next. Finally from the Zenith there are the relieving words: *"The Soviet ships appear to be turning around."* Life resumes; time resumes.

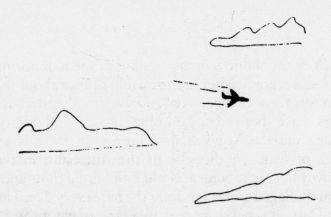

Miscellaneous images: in high school – Sentinel Senior Secondary, West Vancouver, British Columbia – up on the mountain overlooking the city of Vancouver, in physics class hearing a jet pass overhead, turning around surreptitiously and waiting for the pulse of light to crush the city.

At the age of eight: hearing the sirens wail at the corner of Stevens Drive and Bonnymuir Drive in a civil defense drill, and noticing that nobody seemed to care.

The 1970s and disaster movies: seeing *The Poseidon Adventure* for the first time – the first movie I venture downtown, to see on my own at the Orpheum Theater to watch a world tip upside down. *Earthquake*; *The Omega Man*; *The Andromeda Strain*; *Soylent Green*; *Towering Inferno*; *Silent Running*, films nobody makes anymore because they are all projecting so vividly inside our heads – to be among the last people inhabiting worlds that have vanished, ignited, collapsed and been depopulated.

In art school a decade ago I learned that the best way to memorize a landscape is to close your eyes for several seconds and then blink in reverse. That is, open your eyes just briefly, allowing those images before you to burn themselves on to your retina in an instant rather than with an extended gaze. I mention this because this is essentially the same principle that is in operation when one's world is illuminated by the nuclear flash.

This flashing image is a recurring motif in both my everyday thoughts and in my dream life. My most recurring flashing image is of me sitting on the top floor of a 1970s cement apartment building along the ocean waterfront of West Vancouver, on the 20th floor, looking out over the ocean. One of the people in the room with me says, *"Look,"* and I look and see that the sun is growing too large too quickly, like a Jiffy pop popcorn foil dome, glowing orange, like an electric stove element. And then I am awake.

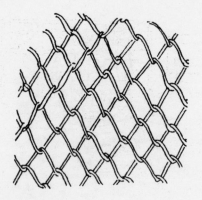

Another recurring image: I am on the high school soccer field in PE class. There is a rumble and as a team we stop kicking the ball and walk over to the chain link fence and look through it to the south, far beyond the horizon to where we know Seattle is supposed to be, 110 miles away. Instead of Seattle we see a pillar of grey dust and rubble pounding on heaven, the earth launched up into the universe, so far up that it will never return – the earth has become the sky.

A third recurring image, very simple: at my parents' house, in their living room looking out through the front window framed by pyrocanthus berries, out at the maple tree on the front lawn; The Flash flashes; I am awake.

When you are young, you always expect that the world is going to end. And then you get older and the world still chugs along and you are forced to re-evaluate your stance on the apocalypse as well as your own relationship to time and death. You realize that the world will indeed continue, with or without you, and the pictures you see in your head. So you try to understand the pictures instead.

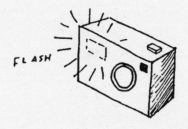

In modern middle-class culture, the absence of death in most people's early years creates a psychic vacuum of sorts. For many, thoughts of a nuclear confrontation are one's first true brush with nonexistence, and because they are the first, they can be the most powerful and indelible. Later in life, more sophisticated equations for death never quite capture that first intensity – the modern sex/death formula; mysterious lumps; the mental illness of friends; the actual death of loved ones – all of life's painful gifts. At least this is what I tell myself to explain these pictures in my head that will not go away.

And these images are more common than I had realized before, and they are not only particular to me. I have asked many of the people I know, and have interviewed many strangers, and I have heard their stories, tales of their blinkings in reverse. And while the pictures vary greatly from one person to the next – some people witness the flash with their family, some with lovers, some with strangers, some with pets, many alone – there is one common thread, and the thread is this: The flash may occur over the tract suburbs of the Fraser River delta, over Richmond and over White Rock; the flash may occur over the Vancouver harbor, over the Strait of Juan de Fuca, over the Pacific Ocean; the flash may occur over the American border, over Seattle, over Bremerton, over Tacoma, Anacortes, and Bellingham. But the Flash – flashing bright, making us remember in an instant what *was*, making us nostalgic before our time – is always flashing to the South – always to the South, up in the sky, up where we know the sun was supposed to have been.

2   The Dead Speak

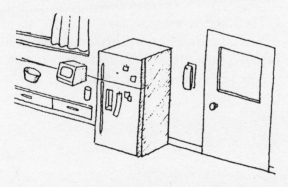

I was by the fridge in the kitchen when it happened.
The phone on the wall next to the fridge rang, and
so I went to pick it up when suddenly the ice maker
began spontaneously chugging out cubes and I thought
that was odd. Then a cupboard door opened by itself,
revealing the dishes inside – and then the power in the
overhead light surged. The game show playing on the
countertop TV then suddenly stopped and the screen
displayed color bars with a piercing tone and then for
maybe a second there was a TV news anchorman with
a map of Iceland on the screen behind him. I said
"hello" into the phone, but it went silent and then the
flash hit. A plastic *Simpsons* cup from Burger King
melted sideways on the counter; the black plastic frame
of the TV softened its edges and began dissolving. I
looked at my hand and saw that the telephone was
turning to mud in my palm, and I saw a bit of skin rip
off like strips of chicken fajita. And then the pulse

occurred. The kitchen window blew inward, all bright and sparkling, like tinsel on a Christmas tree, and the blender crashed into the wall and the Post-it notes on the fridge ignited and then I was dead.

90

I was having my hair done when it happened.

I was around the corner from the salon's front section and I saw the flash in my mirror first. One of the girls up front, Sasha, dropped a coffee cup and held her forearm to her face and screamed and a few of the girls fell to the floor, but I was frozen and could only watch. Like many people, I thought the flash was lightning – but I knew it couldn't have been, because it had been a sunny day. I was thinking this when I saw the potted fig tree by the main windows rustle and burst into flames and the pyramid of Vidal Sassoon shampoo plastic bottles beside the cash register melt and trickle down off the counter. The sprinkler system activated and showered the salon with rain, which turned to steam, and this lasted maybe a second before the blast occurred, caving in the front windows, launching a yellow Corvette and burning pedestrians through the shattered glass, everything smashing into the rear wall by the washing sinks. I don't remember sound, but there must have been some after Sasha screamed. I remember the brown plastic cape melting over Laura's skeleton like cheese on a hamburger; the smell of burning hair – mine, I suppose – and the cinder block walls falling down on me, so in the end it was the collapsing wall that killed me, not the heat or the shock wave.

I was in rush hour gridlock traffic in the middle of the three express lanes leaving the city when it happened.

I had the radio on and was scanning the FM stations, but suddenly it wouldn't pick up any signals and I thought it was broken, so I kept fiddling with the buttons with my head down by the dashboard level. Just then, many of the cars around me began honking and one car jumped out of the right lane and began driving on the meridian. On the radio a woman's voice then began discussing "strategic" events over Baffin Island and northern Minnesota and just then the flash hit, quickly, flaring silently in a second, but my eyes had to readjust afterward, like when the light turns off after being in a sun bed. When my eyes readjusted, the convertible roof of the Mazda Miata two cars ahead of me was on fire, and the cedar trees on the side of the road and the tires of all the cars were smoking and burning and I didn't even have time to duck down before the pulse hit and our cars all jumped forward, like bottles on a table thumped by a drunk, and the coffee from my dashtop holder sprayed on to the windshield and made a scorching sound. My car then hopscotched through the air and on to the rear of a burning Acura Legend and the windshield glass shattered. Noise? A roar, I guess; it happens so fast. My windows were open and I faced the downtown core, and the wind storm was headed toward me – two motorcyclists floating like helium balloons, a telephone booth, fragments of cars and trees; smaller cars – a Mitsubishi I remember, with a dead young woman in the driver's seat, her neck obviously broken and flailing with a set of pearls, her hair gone, her briefcase falling out the window. I remember these small details. I remember it was hard to breathe, like being in a sauna. And I remember a tractor-trailer rig smashing into my car and I remember my roof buckling, and then I was dead.

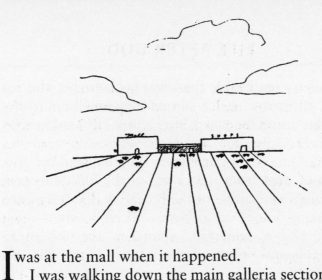

I was at the mall when it happened.

I was walking down the main galleria section with the two kids who were whining to go back and see the animals in the pet shop, but I had so much I had to do that afternoon that I couldn't let them. Amy was tugging at my sleeve and I think I was about to yell at her when the flash occurred and we all looked at the glass ceiling above us – stupid, I know – where the decorative kites had ignited like Kleenex and the glass and metal frame structure was already sagging. I remember being relieved that we were too deep inside the mall to feel the direct heat blast effects. It's amazing the thoughts one can think in such little time – and there was a jet in the sky, and it was a pure coincidence we got to see it, tumbling over, spinning like a petulantly tossed away toy. I yelled, "Fall down!" to the kids, but they were mesmerized by the burning sky above, and I pulled down on their jackets and they fell on their bottoms when the blast hit. The top level of the galleria leapfrogged sideways, like a big slice of bread, cutting off much of our sun. And I remember the contents of the upper level stores falling down on to us below, the shoes and tables and coffee machines and sweaters, like a purse being emptied, and the grey clouds of dust from the center of the blast shooting over what was visible of the outer sky, like grey cake icing being smoothed above us. There was a rushing sound, like a waterfall, and then the reinforced concrete beams began to fall and I tried to grab the kids and dodge the beams, but they came from above and behind us, and the noise was so loud, and there was so little light and the sky was thick with dust and clothing and chocolate chip cookies and price tags and broken glass and blood that it was hard to do anything. And it was then that the oxygen began to be sucked out of the air and it became impossible to breathe. So in the end it was suffocation that I died from.

I was in the office and it was near the end of the day
and people were getting ready to go home when it
happened.

Ellen in the workstation next to me groaned that the
computers had just crashed again, and I looked at my
IBM and it had blanked, too. I was walking over
toward her workstation and she was calling for Ricky,
our in-office computer expert, when the power failed
and we were all looking around in that first confusing
moment when the lights went out, when the flash
occurred: titanium white light, like a Xerox copying
with a raised lid. The flash came from the main bank of
windows across the office, nearer the lunchroom, and
I saw Brent and Tracy headed our way, glowing red,
because the light rays and the gamma rays had passed
through their bodies, lighting them up from the inside
like aborted embryos. Just after the light had flashed,
Tracy then fell to her knees and Brent collapsed over an
office chair. Ellen and I were just starting to go over to

them when the blast hit, like a bursting dam, crashing through the windows, shooting Brent and Tracy and all office furniture in its wake, straight out the window on the other side of the building, on to the employee parking lot. I was pulled over in that direction, too, and I grabbed on to a sound baffle, which was singed black and smoking, and I remember seeing a computer bank wobbling on the edge of the now-gone window, as though trying to decide whether to jump or not, then falling, taking a tangle of power cords with it. I remember Tracy grabbing for me, as she was being helplessly sucked out of the building, blood leaking from her ears, her hair pulled back, a bottle of Liquid Paper exploding against her skull, and I remember reaching for her hand and holding on to it as we were sucked out the building, and then dying together. Somewhere up in the sky.

We are not with you anymore.

It is much later on, now. Please, take your breath, for breath is what *you* require – oxygen, light and water. And time. But not us. We are no longer with you. We are no longer a part of the living. The birds are here with us now – this is where they went. And the fish in the sea – and the plants and all of God's fine animals.

It is cooler here, too, and it is quiet. And we are changed souls; we don't look at things the same way anymore. For there was once a time when we expected the worst. But then the worst happened, did it not? And so we will never be surprised ever again.

GETTYSBURG

Your mother and I honeymooned like bandits in a beat-up 1978 Monte Carlo rental wreck. We stayed in flophouse motels up and down the Appalachian mountains and imagined ourselves as criminals lost in a life of crime – capturing satellites, pulling televangelism scams and climbing down the glass facade of Caesar's Palace while hoisting Adidas bags full of stolen diamonds. In North Carolina we bought a gun and shot at road signs; instead of bathing we sprayed Calvin Klein's Eternity into our armpits; we lost money at church bingos and ate catfish deep-fried in lard. It was ten days of not having to be ourselves, of being invisible and free, of hoping that the childishness of our ways would cancel out the adultness of having gotten married.

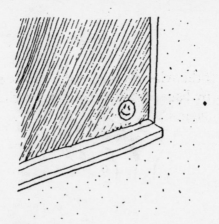

You, yourself, were conceived with love in a cheap motel somewhere in those first few days. Your mother had stopped using birth control on our wedding night and was determined to conceive immediately. On that first night in a motel somewhere in West Virginia she ordered me to keep the curtains open as we consummated our marriage and then afterward told me of her first childhood sexual experience – of peeking into a second-story motel room window one morning while her family was visiting Disneyland, and seeing two honeymooners making love, the woman astride the man, her arms leaning back, her back arched and her rocking breasts shooting skyward. In the middle of watching this uninhibited scene, your mother's father honked the station wagon's horn and she had had to leave for downstairs. But then another delay kept the car stuck in the parking lot so your mother snuck back up to the second floor – only to find the curtains closed and, in the corner of the window where she had been peeking, a small Happy Face carved in the glass with a diamond engagement ring.

During that honeymoon trip we also visited Gettysburg, a site I had always wanted to visit, but one which did not thrill your mother who sulked among the many gift shops while I wandered through the monuments and the graveyard, thinking of the past, of war, of time's odd flow and of respect for finer ideas. I felt solemn; I don't think your mother wanted the mood of the week clouded by anything larger than our own small happiness.

Afterward when I returned to the car, I found that your mother had bought you that gingerbread dolls' house you love so much – the house of a townsman's family – as well as some small furniture and some rag dolls to live inside it. I think she knew even then that she was pregnant with you.

I am reminiscing here. Forgive me. My mood is everywhere today, like the weather. The sky is doing four things at once – raining, hailing, sunning and, it would seem further up on Grouse Mountain, snowing. It just doesn't know what to do.

And here is why my mind is all over the place: your mother left me a week ago and she took you with her.

She phones me from her mother's house and we talk every day. This is better than nothing. She says she has fallen out of love with me. She says she is confused. She says she feels lost, sort of like the way she felt when she was younger.

I told her that everybody feels lost when they're young.

But she says there's a difference. She tells me that at least when she was younger she felt lost in her own special way. Now she just feels lost like everyone else.

I asked her if she was unhappy; she says it is not a question of happiness. She says she remembers another thing about when she was young – she remembers when the world was full of wonder – when life was a strand of magic moments strung together, a succession of mysteries revealed, leaving her feeling as though she was in a trance. She remembers back when all it took to make her feel like she was a part of the stars was to simply talk about things like death and life and the universe. She doesn't know how to reclaim that sense of magic anymore.

I told her to wait – that maybe this is about something else.

She says she doesn't want us to become dreadful people who do dreadful things to each other because there will be no one to forgive us. She tries to use a brave, cheerful voice with me, but it never lasts long. She says she can't live in a marriage without romantic love.

I tried to joke with her. I told her that in the beginning of all relationships you're out there bungee jumping every weekend but after six months you're renting videos and buying corn chips just like everyone else – and the next day you can't even remember what video you rented.

Our calls last a little while. And then she will hang up and I am alone again and try to understand what she is telling me. I try to figure out where this change in her came from. I walk through the house but it now makes no sense – stairs run into the ceiling; rooms are walled off. Perhaps I clean up some of your remaining toys, absentmindedly trying your Fisher Price McDonald's employee headset. The phone will maybe ring again or sometimes it will leave me lonely for the night.

I sit at the kitchen table in my flannel housecoat eating toast with peanut butter while I think these thoughts. The neighbor's German shepherd barks at ghosts and the occasional redneck guns an engine down Lonsdale Avenue a few blocks away. But otherwise the world is quiet here in this unassuming grey-and-pink 1950s box which overlooks the lights of the ships in the harbor and the tall buildings downtown.

Now: I am an affectionate man but I have much trouble showing it.

When I was younger I used to worry so much about being alone – of being unlovable or incapable of love. As the years went on, my worries changed. I worried that I had become incapable of having a relationship, of offering intimacy. I felt as though the world lived inside a warm house at night and I was outside, and I couldn't be seen – because I was out there in the night. But now I am inside that house and it feels just the same.

Being alone here now, all of my old fears are erupting – the fears I thought I had buried forever by getting married: fear of loneliness; fear that being in and out of love too many times itself makes you harder to love; fear that I would never experience real love; fear that someone would fall in love with me, get extremely close, learn everything about me and then pull the plug; fear that love is only important up until a certain point after which everything is negotiable.

For so many years I lived a life of solitude and I thought life was fine. But I knew that unless I explored intimacy and shared intimacy with someone else then life would never progress beyond a certain point. I remember thinking that unless I knew what was going on inside of someone else's head other than my own I was going to explode.

The phone rings. It's her. I tell her a thought I have
had. I tell her how strange it is that we're trapped
inside our bodies for seventy-odd years and never once
in all that time can we just, say, park our bodies in a
cave for even a five-minute break and float free from
the bonds of Earth. I then tell her about the fears I had
years ago. I tell her that I thought that intimacy with
another soul was the closest I could ever come to
leaving my body.

She says to me, but were we ever intimate? How
intimate were we *really*? Sure, there were the ordinary
familiarity-type things – our bodies, our bodily dis-
charges and stains and seepages, an encyclopedic
knowledge of each other's family grudges, knowledge
of each other's early school yard slights, our dietary
peccadilloes, our TV remote control channel-changing
styles. And yet . . .

And yet?

And yet in the end did we ever really give each other

completely to the other? Do either of us even know how to really share ourselves? Imagine the house is on fire and I reach to save that one thing – what is it? Do you know? Imagine that I am drowning and I reach within myself to save that one memory which is me – what is it? Do you know? What things would either of us reach for? Neither of us knows. After all these years we just wouldn't know.

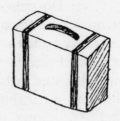

You were born almost ten months to the day after the wedding, wildly overdue. And once you were born, almost magically our life was converted from one of carefree penury to one of striving middle-class participation. One thing about having kids, o daughter of mine, is that even the most anarchistic paupers suddenly find themselves living in a house. Parents begin slipping you checks; strangers in the Shoppers Drug Mart checkout line earnestly speak to you about the importance of growing up while you wait to pay for a breast pump. The process is seductive. But in the end *you're* the one who has to pay the mortgage. Society indeed conspires to keep you ball-and-chained.

And let me tell you a bit more about my life now – brace yourself, for it's not glamorous: I travel the roads. I work for a medium-sized software company called ImmuDyne. I am not an egghead – I'm just a guy in a suit who drives a boring mid-sized car and spends too much time in airport hubs with a suitcase full of brochures, diskettes, smoker's toothpaste and airline honey-roasted nuts which I eat in over-air-conditioned hotel rooms while watching late-night TV. I feel like the punch line to a joke I might have told you ten years ago. But you know: life just catches up on you.

When you're young, you always feel that life hasn't yet begun – that "life" is always scheduled to begin next week, next month, next year, after the holidays – whenever. But then suddenly you're old and the scheduled life didn't arrive. You find yourself asking, "Well then, exactly what was it I was having – that interlude – that scrambly madness – all that time I had before?"

Another afternoon: I'm unshaven, dishes are fermenting in the kitchen sink and my shirt smells like a teenage boy's bedroom. There were no clean spoons around the house so I ate cottage cheese with a plastic tortoiseshell shoehorn that was lying next to the couch – so I guess I've hit a new personal low.

The TV's off; before me is a coffee mug full of dying felt pens and three-ring binder paper left over from my stress-management night school class two years ago. Rain is dripping on the laurel leaves out the front window. Looking there, I remember your mother once sitting on the window sill, eating Sweet Tarts and talking to the barn swallows nesting in the rafters above. I remember your mother flashdancing with a kitchen chair she had nicknamed "Otis" one New Year's Eve. These little things make us love people and yet realize at the same time how little we know them.

Gettysburg

I don't know what it was about myself that your mother found lovable. I guess whatever it was is not enough to overcome the things she is feeling now.

I am a quiet man. I tend to think things through and try not to say too much. But here I am, saying perhaps too much. But there are these feelings inside me which need badly to escape, I guess. And this makes me feel relieved because one of my big concerns these past few years is that I've been losing my ability to feel things with the same intensity – the way I felt when I was younger. It's scary – to feel your emotions floating away and just not caring. I guess what's really scary is not caring about the loss. I guess this is what your mother is responding to. I make a note in my mind to talk about this with her.

A phone call: I tell your mother that I know I've been feeling less these days but I promise that I'll try to feel more. She laughs, not meanly, but genuinely.

I say that I know life has gotten so boring so quickly in so many ways – and that neither of us planned for this to happen. I never thought that we would end up in the suburbs with lawnmowers and swing sets. I never thought that I'd be a lifer at some useless company. But then wasn't this the way of the world? The way of adulthood, of maturity, of bringing up children?

I am kicked in the gut. She says that one of the cruelest things you can do to another person is pretend that you care about them more than you really do. I'm not sure if she means this about me or if she means this about herself. I ask her and she says she doesn't know.

She says: I'm sorry, but I just stopped being in love. It happened. I woke up and it was gone and it scared me and I felt like I was lying and hollow pretending to

119

be "the wife." And I just can't do it anymore. I love you but I'm not in love.

I say: But I still love *you*.

She says: *Do* you? *Really?*

I say: Yes.

She says: Then I'm hurting you. Please stop asking me to say these things to you.

Why is it so hard to quickly sum up all of those things that we have learned while being alive here on Earth? Why can't I just tell you, *"In ten minutes you are going to be hit by a bus, and so in those ten minutes you must quickly itemize what you have learned from being alive."*

Chances are that you would have a blank list. And even if you gave the matter great concentration, you would probably still have a blank list. And yet we *know* in our hearts that we learn the greatest and most profound things by breathing, by seeing, by feeling, by falling in and out and in and out of love.

121

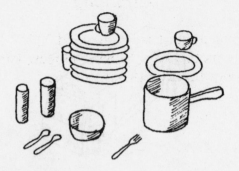

My mother comes to visit and she talks while she washes my dishes. She does not see things the way I do. She says that your mother is young and will see things differently after a while. Just hang in there. She says that what we are going through is common in couples and one of the great sad points of life – but it is survivable. I don't ask her how she knows this because I might be even more saddened by the answer.

She scrubs and puts order into the chaos. She says: "First there is love, then there is disenchantment and then there is the rest of your life."

And I say, "But what *about* the rest of your life – what about all the time that remains?"

And she says, "Oh – there's friendship. Or at least familiarity. And there's safety. And after that there's sleep."

I think to myself: How do any of us know that it's going to end up like this? That *this* is all there was maybe going to be? I say, "Oh, God."

And my mother says to me, "Honey, God is what keeps us together after the life is gone."

You are old enough to enjoy stories, now, Baby, so let me tell you a story. Let me tell you a story about Gettysburg – honeymoonland – of a man from the town of Gettysburg itself, called into duty days after the battle, to clean up the remains – rolling up his sleeves and gathering the slain bodies, row upon row, digging graves in an endless line, building bonfires of broken horses and broken mules, breathing clouds of flies and the steam of blood and soil, burying and exhuming, burying and exhuming the rows of bodies and limbs, all day long for many days in succession.

He returns to his home and he is unable to speak, and he sits by the fireplace. His daughters surround him but are silenced to a hush by their mother. They know that this is not the way he used to be. The children whisper, "Why won't Daddy talk?" and the mother says, "That is a father's choice, children," but Mother herself is worried, but then what can she say to him, either?

Gettysburg

She whisks her daughters off to bed, their toys left behind them on the floor, and then goes off to bed herself, taking a long look back into the main room at her husband, still seated by the fire, still silent.

The night passes and the children awaken. They run downstairs and there, while the birds sing outside and a wind blows through an open window, they find their father lying asleep in his chair next to the fireplace embers. They are happy that he is resting and they go to their breakfast. It is only later on when they go to play that they realize that something is different, but they don't know exactly what, and so they give the matter no second thought, laughing with each other and reaching for their dolls which they find lined up in neat rows up against the side of the dolls' house.

IN THE DESERT

You are
the first generation
raised
without
religion

For Michael Stipe

Clark County, Nevada
San Bernardino County, California
Riverside County, California

I had been driving south from Las Vegas to Palm Springs and the Nothingness was very much on my mind. I kept on being surprised by the bigness of the landscape – just how far *nothing* can extend to – in my rental car, climbing up and falling down the slopes and sinks of the Mojave desert, counting the Rothkos of skid marks of long-dead car collisions on Interstate 15's white cement lanes, watching an old woman apply lipstick inside a Lincoln Town Car while a man at the wheel coughed up oysters, just past the Hoover Dam offramp.

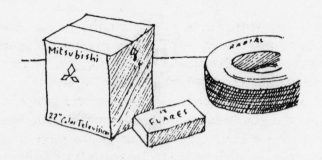

It was around noon and some tired wisps of cloud hazed the sun and it was not warm outside. On the seat beside me sat a lukewarm nearly empty bottle of Gatorade, an improperly folded map of Nevada and some unplayed chips from the Showboat Casino; in the trunk was a cardboard Mitsubishi 27″ TV box whose contents were both too illegal and too shameful to mention here.

The car radio's SEEK button was continuously prowling for new stations. Quirks in the Van Allen radiation belts allowed me to receive radio stations from all over the West – those fragments of cultural memory and information that compose the invisible information structure I consider my real home – my virtual community. I was hearing the sort of information that I knew would make me homesick if I were stuck in Europe or dying in Vietnam: it was 61° in San Francisco and 58° in Daly City; a Christian talk show from Las Vegas asked listeners to pray for a housewife with lupus; traffic on the Santa Monica Freeway was frozen owing to an overturned propane tanker at the Normandie onramp; the Mayor of Albuquerque was accepting listener phone-ins.

I was on the Interstate 15 somewhere between the blink-and-you-miss-it town of Jean and the gaudy casinoplex at State Line. Outside the car there were no trees or billboards or plants or animals or buildings – not even fences – just radio waves and the Mojave's volcanic granite, experienced at seventy-seven miles per hour.

It was also my birthday – I remember that – 31, and I also remember that I wasn't feeling lonely even though it was my birthday and I was alone and I was in the middle of nowhere. A few years previously, a similar situation would have had me sweaty with anxiety, but loneliness had of late become an emotion I had stopped feeling so intensely. I had learned loneliness's extremes and had mapped its boundaries; loneliness was no longer something new or frightening – just another aspect of life that, once identified, seemed to disappear. But I realized a capacity for not feeling lonely carried a very real price, which was the threat of feeling nothing at all. Perhaps the nothingness outside was trying to seep into the car in whatever way it could. I rolled up my window even though I knew it was rolled up as high as possible already and again pressed the SEEK button.

I will now tell you what was in the Mitsubishi cardboard box: 2,000 syringes stolen from a Kaiser Permanente hospital in North Las Vegas plus 1,440 ampules of 50cc Parastolin anabolic steroids smuggled up from Mexico. I was to deliver this box to a private physical trainer of TV celebrities named Oscar who lived in the Las Palmas neighborhood of Palm Springs.

Now, I believe you own your body outright, so what you do with it is your own business. I therefore do not have a moral problem with steroid usage, but I recognize the fact that many people *do*. And of course I know that steroids are illegal, and that shooting up with used needles is a common channel of HIV transmission. Actually, it was precisely because of the HIV transmission business that I thought I was doing a good deed – by providing clean syringes to the bodybuilding community of the American Southwest. But this is a moral fine point that is not up for discussion here. The point is that the syringes were stolen, and while I did not actually steal them myself, were I to be somehow apprehended, I would be considered an accessory. I didn't even want to *begin* imagining what would happen to me if this happened because my own criminal record, while not entirely shocking, is not entirely lily white.

I could hear the ampules tinkling in the trunk while I hummed along to an old Four Lads song on a station that warbled in from Salt Lake City. I was in the middle of the three-lane highway in between the speeding lane and the truck-lane. My engine was pleasingly silent. I sang loudly and forced myself to listen to my voice: flat and hopefully generic, for I have always tried to speak with a voice that has no regional character – a voice from nowhere. This is because I have never really felt like I was "from" anywhere; home to me, as I have said, is a shared electronic dream of cartoon memories, half-hour sitcoms and national tragedies. I have always prided myself on my lack of accent – my lack of any discernible regional flavor. I used to think mine was a Pacific Northwest accent, from where I grew up, but then I realized my accent was simply the accent of nowhere – the accent of a person who has no fixed home in their mind.

Here's what was on my mind: I had recently begun worrying about my feelings disappearing more and more – noticing that I had seemed to simply be feeling less and less. These worries became more focused and stronger as I was driving. I felt like I was turning into a reptile, an iguana sitting on a rock with a decaying memory and no compassion. I thought of the TV stars Oscar terrorizes with his fitness routines, the old ones with sagging leathery cheeks, the ones who have seen everything, twice, but who still smile for the paparazzi on the sidewalk outside the Century City Cineplex Odeon – reptiles for whom life has been serial betrayal since the dawn of television. I figure that's what people become as they age: reptiles; these old TV stars are merely the amplified version.

My drive continued and worries about vanishing feelings remained like a background radiation. But I guess the nice thing about driving a car is that the physical act of driving itself occupies a good chunk of brain cells that otherwise would be giving you trouble overloading your thinking. New scenery continually erases what came before; memory is lost, shuffled, relabeled and forgotten. Gum is chewed; buttons are pushed; windows are lowered and opened. A fast moving car is the only place where you're legally allowed to not deal with your problems. It's enforced mediation and this is good.

A dirty black Camaro passed my car, driven by Debbie, pagan goddess of Dairy Queens. A radio station vanished, and another from Yuma replaced it: gospel tunes. The static was bad.

I began wondering exactly what was lying at the end of the road for me, in all senses of the word. There was nobody waiting for me in Palm Springs; Oscar was in Beverly Hills until tomorrow and he hardly counted. Nor was there anybody waiting for me anywhere, for that matter.

I was wondering what was the logical end product of this recent business of my feeling less and less. Is feeling nothing the inevitable end result of *believing* in nothing? And then I got to feeling frightened – thinking that there might not actually *be* anything to believe in, in particular. I thought it would be such a sick joke to have to remain alive for decades and not believe in or feel anything.

A mobile home was stalled on the road's shoulder.

Off to the right, to the north, fighter jets from Nellis Air Force Base braided together their vapor trails.

I began to wonder what exactly I had believed in up until now that had allowed me to reach my present emotional circumstance. This is not an easy thing to do. Precisely articulating one's beliefs is difficult. My own task had been made more difficult because I had been raised without religion by parents who had broken their own pasts and moved to the West Coast – who had raised their children clean of any ideology in a cantilevered modern house overlooking the Pacific Ocean – at the end of history, or so they had wanted to believe.

I tried to forget what I was thinking about and just listen to the radio. On it there was a story of an Arizona man who was shot in the head, but who, in the hospital waiting room, sneezed out the bullet which had lodged in his sinus cavity, and which fell with a clink on to the shiny black floor.

There was the story of a central California widow who had fought to have her recently dead husband exhumed, pleading her case that before he had died he had swallowed her diamond ring in some sort of spite and that she wanted this jewel returned. But in the end she confessed that she had not slept for many many weeks and that she had been spending her nights lying on his grave, trying to speak to him, and that all she really wanted was just to be able to see his face one more time.

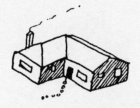

And there was a story of a young child who, upon hearing that his parents were divorcing, had disappeared. A search party had been called out to comb the neighborhood and he was found, two days later, alive, having buried himself within the pink fiberglass insulation of the family's attic, trying to become a part of the house, trying to pretend he was dead.

And there were Christian radio stations, too, so many many stations, and the voices on them seemed so enthusiastic and committed. They sounded like they sincerely believed in what they were saying, and so for once I decided to pay attention to these stations, trying to figure out what exactly it was they were believing in, trying to understand the notion of Belief.

The stations talked about Jesus and salvation and I found it was pretty hard listening because these religious types are always so whacked out and extreme. I think they take things too literally and miss too many points because of this literalism. This had always been the basic flaw with religion – or so I had been taught, and so (I realized) I had come to believe. So at least I knew *one* thing for sure that I believed in.

The radio stations all seemed to be talking about Jesus nonstop, and it seemed to be this crazy orgy of projection, with everyone projecting on to Jesus the antidotes to the things that had gone wrong in their own lives. He is Love. He is Forgiveness. He is Compassion. He is a Wise Career Decision. He is a Child Who Loves Me.

I was feeling a sense of loss as I heard these people. I felt like Jesus was sex – or rather, I felt like I was from another world where sex did not exist and I arrived on Earth and everyone talked about how good sex felt, and showed me their pornography and built their lives around sex, and yet I was forever cut off from the true sexual experience. I did not deny that the existence of Jesus was real to these people – it was merely that I was cut off from their experience in a way that was never connectable.

And yet I had to ask myself over and over what it was that these radio people were seeing in the face of Jesus. They sounded like their lives had once been so messed up and lost as they spoke; at least they were no longer so lost anymore – like AA people. So I figured that was a good thing.

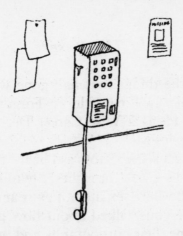

These thoughts were all occurring after I had crested the Halloran Summit and was descending down the Shadow Mountains into the town of Baker, a truck stop oasis where I pulled over and ordered a hamburger and strawberry pie at the Bun Boy restaurant, home of the World's Largest Thermometer: 134 ft tall and digitally displaying 54°. While waiting for my food to arrive I made phone calls from the Pacific Bell booth next to the washrooms. I returned a message on my Las Vegas answering machine from Laurelle, who operates a jai alai court near the Fremont. The first thing she did was ask me my birthday. When I gave her that particular day's date, she didn't make the connection or wish me a happy birthday or anything. She instead read me my horoscope and then she told me the news, that Oscar had been busted in North Hollywood and the cops would most likely be on my tail as a result.

My chest constricted; my brain stem caught fire. Suffice it to say, the main imperative at the moment

150

became to ditch the boxes of Parastolin and syringes as soon as possible. But simply disposing the boxes right there in the public trash cans in the town of Baker was out of the question. The place was like a *Twilight Zone* episode, and riddled with cops – two cops for every diner: there were CHiPS, there were San Bernardino County sheriffs, and there were even two guys from the forestry service which was such a joke because there couldn't have been a tree for fifty miles in any direction.

Ordinary trash cans themselves were out of the question – my fingerprints were all over everything, anyway, and what if some busybody were to find them? The only method of disposal, I figured, was to bury the syringes somewhere further down the road. Fortunately my car was a rental and so the police wouldn't know to look for it in particular. As long as I drove the speed limit, everything was cool and I could consider what to do with my boxes of loot.

I continued my drive to Palm Springs via Barstow and San Bernardino and looped around east and on to Interstate 10. I was indeed feeling many things – panic mostly – and I chewed too many sticks of Freedent gum and turned off the radio and completely forgot to resume those thoughts I had been thinking as I descended into the valley before lunch, my thoughts about the face of Jesus. I thought instead of my growling stomach and regretted leaving my lunch on

151

the counter back at the Bun Boy after my hasty exit. All I had had to eat all day was half a cherry Pop-Tart and a cup of coffee back in Las Vegas.

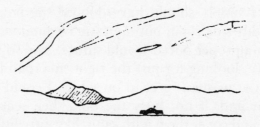

Two hours later I was about ten miles out of Palm Springs, pulling off the Indian Avenue freeway exit in the opposite direction of town, in pursuit of a steroid burial spot. From shotgun practice I roughly remembered the desert and gulches between Desert Hot Springs and Thousand Palms; I figured that area would probably best suit my purposes – a meaner, sparser part of the desert, on the eastern side of the San Andreas fault, where citizens kited checks and drove in cars in which windows had been lost long ago and replaced with plastic bags. People there were probably less inclined to ask any questions about anything out of the normal.

I was a bit frazzled from the long drive. My shirt felt sweaty and dirty – car sweat. And I was cranky, too, or rather, I would have been cranky if people had been near me. Sometimes you can't realize you're in a bad mood until another person enters your orbit.

My sense of reason also seemed to have dwindled. I

suppose I simply should have ditched the box along any old dirt side road, but my state of mind was such that only a proper burial would suffice. And so I drove and drove, looking for just the right side road leading off into the wastes – a road on which I could simply disappear and, if not bury the box, then scatter the contents and cover them with sand, like kitty litter. But even out there in the center of nowhere there was always a car zooming by in the distance that might see me. I had to drive a far way out before I could be confident of not being discovered dumping my cargo.

The road I finally found was twisty, with shoulders littered with shotgun shell casings and smashed beer bottles. It ran down an ignored, very wide and low canyon. From it stemmed a variety of forks leading into an array of smaller Joshua tree-specked crevasses and washes. To judge from the occasional desiccated mattresses, broken couches and refrigerators around me, others had passed this way with similar notions of disposal.

It felt good to be driving at a speed other than seventy-five miles per hour, and over real earth, not just cement and pavement, so I drove farther than I should have. When I reached the end of the road I had chosen – a path, almost – I stopped the car and got out to stretch. I surveyed my dumping spot: ugly and barren and boxed off from view from anywhere else.

I opened the trunk and removed the Mitsubishi carton, spraying the contents on to the sand to the side of the car. I ripped off the flaps and molded a spatula, scooping sand on top of the white syringe wrapping papers, watching the last of the glass Parastolin ampules gleam under the late afternoon sun.

My movements were jerky, and I could feel my bloodstream having a major sugar crash. I was angry that I had forgotten to feed myself because in general, once I get too hungry I become very angry. I knew that even if I hurried to the nearest gas station and got some emergency crap food, that would still be a half hour away.

From this, one can imagine how badly I reacted when the car didn't start when I turned the key in the ignition. Happy fucking birthday asshole. I couldn't believe my luck. I looked under the hood, but the engine bore no resemblance to the V8's I'd remembered from my teenage years. The realization hit me in a lightning crack of anger that I had no choice but to walk back to the main road, and from there probably walk the *entire* way back into the nearest phone or convenience store. Nobody gives rides to lone males walking through the desert. Fuck.

And so my walk began. It did not begin well, and it quickly worsened. There was only a little sun left and once it went behind the San Gorgonio mountains the lights would be out completely. A swarm of tweeze-resistant prickly burrs decided to infest the tops of my socks. The air was windy and chilly and would only grow more so. I was thirsty, I was ravenous with hunger and quickly went from anger to confusion and mild dizziness.

My arms were crossed, I was muttering fucks and shits under my breath, and then after a while I just shut up and tried to walk with a blank head – trying to make time disappear by pretending time no longer existed. And this fake Zen continued until I realized after maybe an hour of not getting anywhere, that I had taken a wrong fork somewhere back – I had walked who-knows-how-far on the wrong road.

I was the biggest loser in the world. I couldn't even get mad. I groaned with despair, not even knowing if retracing my path would make any difference because I wasn't sure where the correct forks were.

So I sat down on a rock to sharpen my wits as well as to huddle and keep my warmth in. I watched the sunlight fade on schedule. I then turned and walked back in the direction I had come from, mechanically pushing myself along, having no other option, not having the faintest idea what road I was on, getting more and more fatalistic about what might happen to me.

This went on for some hours, by which time the sky had long been fully dark and fully cold. And on top of the stick-insect discomfort, the boredom and endlessness of the walk, I was spooked by the basic darkness of night. I was considering all sorts of scenarios one might encounter in the desert – rampaging bikers cartooned on angel dust; snuff movies in progress, being filmed with shotguns pointed at unwanted visitors; rattlers slithering over abandoned heatless murdered bodies. I thought of what an unglamorous end to my life to simply be terminated out here in the emptiness. I wanted to be in a city or a town – a community – *any* community. And so I was in this woeful state, when an event occurred that made me lose my breath – I became aware that there was another person walking behind me.

At first I thought the footsteps might be echoes of my own, but then my subconscious realized the steps I heard were out of synch with mine. My walk's pace skipped a tiny beat and a keen observer would have realized that something had changed in my demeanor, that my body language revealed I had sensed a danger of some sort.

The steps I heard were, I figured, about a stone's throw away, faintly crunchy like the sound of Cocoa Pebbles being chewed across a table. And because the steps were faster than mine, I knew The Stepper was gaining on me.

And so the shadow grew larger, almost to full size. I saw a hunched man's figure with a backpack of urethane foam battened down with bungie cords and flattened McDonald's white paper bags. He had a white Spanish moss beard and a plaid shirt and green Dickies work pants that were so worn they were shiny. He was a drifter – a desert rat – like the ones who occasionally haunt the Desert Fashion Plaza, visibly frighteningly suntanned even in the dark of three-quarter moonlight, with skin like beef jerky, pores like a salt and pepper shaker and milky hints of cataracts in both eyes. He walked toward me and I guardedly said, *"Hello"* once more. He then stopped short of me, as though we had met casually outside a Radio Shack or something. He said in a voice rich with phlegm and years of desert monologues: *"I walk out here almost very night, but tonight there won't be rain, and so we're fine."* His breath was like fire; like pepper.

My relief was great; he was mad but not harmful –

too poor even for weapons. Even in my dilapidated condition, I could take him in a scrap. It was my turn to talk. I said, "Rain? No – I guess not."

In retrospect it was quite idiotic. I was trying to be casual about this decidedly odd encounter and he was simply too crazy to perceive it as even being odd. I was trying to pretend we were meeting each other under sunlight, not moonlight; I was trying to give our situation a comfortable guy-like dignity, like two models chatting in a J. Crew catalogue.

My drifter pal then made a shrug with a dirty left shoulder, spat a gob and indicated that we continue walking. My legs now wobbled, mainly from my lack of blood sugar. Walking together quickly erased much of what fear remained. The drifter didn't even question the fact that a person might be walking lost in the desert at night – as though lost strolls were the most natural activity on earth.

And he wasn't really talking to me, either – he was broadcasting – like a cheap AM radio station that had come through on the SEEK button. I wish I could say that we talked about simple things while we walked, too – that he offered me salt-of-the-earth insight into life – wisdom garnered from all his years of drifting. But he didn't. He never even volunteered his name and I never volunteered mine. He talked some more about the evening's rainfall that was never to arrive. He talked about a Republican conspiracy; about the Colorado River; about Princess Caroline of Monaco. I only half paid attention to his words, as though I was driving. He told me he was walking to Indio. He asked me, "Now where'd *you* be headin' for a stroll?"

I replied without much energy that I was trying to find one of the roads back to Desert Hot Springs, Bermuda Dunes or Palm Springs.

"Well if that's your case," he replied, stopping us in our tracks, "you're walkin' the wrong way."

It was jarring that he actually connected with me here, that he had actually heard my words. I tried to react casually to this. "Oh?"

He stopped and I stopped and he said to me, "Look, whatever you're doin' out here, that's okay. Maybe you didn't want to see me and," he smacked his lips, "maybe I didn't see *you*. But that *there*'s the road you want to be walkin'." He indicated a small "Y" in the road a stone's throw back. "And it's maybe an hour to Dillan Road. Not that you'll be closer to much. Hot Springs, maybe. It's a two-hour walk from there. *Capish?*"

His tone of voice made it clear that it took a strong act of will for him to be able to connect with me as much as he already had. I nodded, and his face dissolved back into its previous craziness.

166

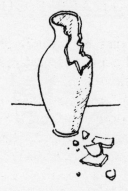

The fact of the matter was that he was simply a very far-gone desert rat. I felt naïve and middle-class for having hoped – even briefly – that I could bond with the unbondable, for thinking that all it takes to make crazy people uncrazy is a little bit of hearty attention and good sense.

And then I felt sad because I realized that once people are broken in certain ways, they can't ever be fixed, and this is something nobody ever tells you when you are young and it never fails to surprise you as you grow older as you see the people in your life break one by one. You wonder when your turn is going to be, or if it's already happened.

And so I stood by him rather dumbly and he twitched. I stared at his backpack like a Labrador dog staring at a dinner table and then I felt badly; I realized I was menacing him with this stare. For the first time, I think he was a bit frightened of meeting me – a stranger – in the middle of nowhere. He reached into the pouch on his back and pulled out two lumps and handed them to me: a microwaveable plastic container of Beefaroni and a cold Baked Apple Pie from McDonald's

"The macaroni's swiped from a 7-Eleven," he said.

I said, "No, *no!*" I wanted to let him know that I wasn't planning to rob him, so I handed him a fifty dollar bill from my shirt pocket which he stuffed, unfolded, into a grubby front pocket. Having done this, he darted away without even saying good-bye, off down the road, vanishing all too soon into the night, leaving me there near the Y in the road, scraping the Beefaroni out of a plastic cup with dusty fingers, eating the Baked Apple Pie without even chewing, knowing that, bad as my situation was, at least it would not be forever.

Now:
There is so much you don't know about me –
things I haven't told you – for instance, that I *do* have
a family, that I believe there is a God, that I was once
a child – and that I have fallen in love twice and that
neither time lasted. But how much of this matters in the
end if you are alone. What is our memory? What is our
history? How much a part of us is the landscape, and
how much are we a part of it?

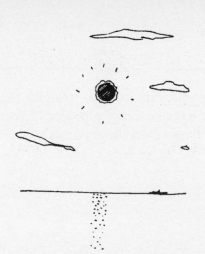

My body grows old, it turns strange colors, refuses orders, becomes less and less a part of the me I remember I once was. I read what I have written here and realize that I am not a happy person and maybe I never will be.

My night in the desert was a few years ago now. Since then I have seen more of this world – I have lived in Los Angeles and seen the fires burn there; I have seen the glaciers in Alaska fall apart and float away into the sea; I have seen an eclipse of the sun from a yacht floating on an ocean thick with crude oil. And with each of these sights I have thought of the damaged face of the drifter in the desert, gone, untraceable, vanished into the wastes outside of Indio, Scottsdale, Las Vegas – his own private planets in his own private universe.

But I talk too much here. Yet how often is it we are rescued by a stranger, if ever at all? And how is it that our lives can become drained of the possibility of forgiveness and kindness – so drained that even one small act of mercy becomes a potent lifelong memory? How do our lives reach these points?

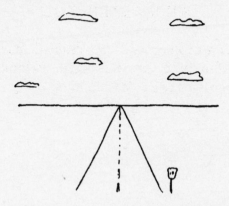

It is with these thoughts in mind that I now see the drifter's windburned face when I now consider my world – his face that reminds me that there is still something left to believe in after there is nothing left to believe in. A face for people like me – who were pushed to the edge of loneliness and who maybe fell off and who when we climbed back on, our world never looked the same.

PATTY HEARST

This past week has gotten me to wondering about life. Well, not life ex*act*ly – but the sequence of life's events. Does, for instance, it matter in life that we travel through our days from A to B to C to D . . . birth to love to marriage to children to death, and so forth? Or is the storyboard aspect of life just some sort of bookkeeping device we're stuck with as humans to try to make sense of our iffy situation here on Earth? As I have said, this past week has gotten me wondering about this.

First of all, there was Walter. Walter was a black Labrador retriever who lived three doors down from my parents' house up on the mountain West Vancouver. A quiet, good-hearted soul, Walter had been visiting our house for many years. He would appear outside the kitchen patio door, woof once, and we would let him inside. He would then amble around the house a bit, his toenails clicking on the linoleum, mooch a scrap or two, and then he would lie on the kitchen floor and be one of the family for a few hours. When it was time for Walter to leave, he would woof again once more, and we would let him out. Walter was all the fun and benefits of a pet without any of the fuss and muss.

Anyway, about a month ago Walter stopped visiting my parents' place. Mom mentioned it to me during a phone call, saying she and Dad were a bit concerned but they didn't know what exactly they should do. Then a few days later their phone rang – it was Mrs. Miller, Walter's owner, saying that her husband had died some weeks previously. My mother expressed condolences to Mrs. Miller, who said the worst of it was over and that her children were being good to her. But one problem she was having, though, was that Walter had become miserable and wasn't his old self anymore. She wondered if we might come over to visit him and try to cheer him up.

Mom rallied the troops. She asked me if I would come over from across town and I said that of course I would. In the end me, Mom, Dad and my younger brother, Brent, the aging film student who never left home, all walked to the Millers' house – Mom with a blueberry-peach pie, me with a box of liver-flavored doggie treats and Brent with a HandyCam with which he recorded our visit.

Mrs. Miller answered the door, we made our greetings and then she showed us into the living room where Walter sat on a Hudson's Bay blanket on the chesterfield with *Wheel of Fortune* playing in the background, looking, for all the world, like a senior citizen. Brent was excited that there was a TV on in the room. I think he thought it made his videoing more arty.

Anyway, when Walter saw us he raised his snout, pricked his ears slightly and gave us a dispirited little wag of his tail, but all of his vim was gone. We turned down the volume on the TV and took seats beside him and patted his head. I gave him a doggie treat, which he nibbled at so as not to make me unhappy – such gracious manners – but otherwise he remained miserable-looking.

We talked to Walter. Brent told him that the Klassens' evil Siamese cat, Ping, had a litter of five kittens but Dad said, no, Ping had had six, and that

Mrs. Klassen didn't know who the father was. And then Dad and Brent got in a squabble over, of all subjects, Ping. Normally the very mention of the cat would have had Walter's neck hairs bristling, but then he merely raised his eyebrows slightly, his chin resting on his forepaws.

After fifteen minutes or so we left the house, telling Walter that he could come and visit us any time and we waved goodbye. Again he gave us a dispirited little thump-thump of his tail and that was the last we saw of him.

Walter died days later – of a broken heart, we all supposed. Brent phoned me up to tell me the news which depressed us both, but Brent said not to be. He tried to make a joke. He said, "Well at least Walter got to go through life with a hip all-black wardrobe."

I said that he and all his trendy art friends were sick. And then he told me to lighten up. He said that duration doesn't mean anything to a dog. Whether you go to the corner store for ten minutes or whether you go to Hawaii for two weeks, all your dog experiences during your absence is a "sadness event" of no fixed duration. "One hour . . . two weeks – it's all the same to your dog. Walter suffered and was miserable, but not the way a person would have suffered."

Brent then said that humans are the only animal able to feel the pain of sorrow that has been stretched out through linear time. He said our curse as humans is that we are trapped in time – our curse is that we are forced to interpret life as a sequence of events – a story

181

– and that when we can't figure out what our particular story is we feel lost somehow. "Dogs only have a present tense in their lives," he continued. "Their memories are like those carved ice swans you see at weddings, that look good but melt in an hour. Humans have to endure everything in life in agonizingly endless clock time – every single second of it. Not only this, but we have to *remember* having endured our entire lives, as well. What a drag, no? It's amazing we all haven't gone mad."

I said that sorrow was sorrow. I said I had to think over what Brent was saying. And I said that I missed Walter in whatever kind of time Brent wanted to talk about, thank you.

Our call ended on a rather testy note, but Brent really did get me to thinking.

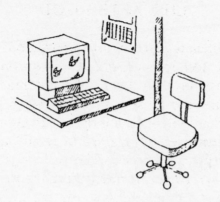

Anyway, there was another event that happened this week that has gotten me wondering about life's strange sequence. An event more important than Walter's dying (though I don't mean to diminish his loss to me). It's just that . . . well – you'll see.

The event was this: I received a phone call from Jeremy, an old high-school friend. Jeremy told me that my sister, Laurie, had been spotted up at Whistler, working at one of that ski resort's convenience stores – not the Husky station, or the Rainbow but one further up the highway. I asked him if he was absolutely *positive* it was Laurie and he replied that he hadn't actually *seen* Laurie him*self*. Rather, a friend of his had made the sighting. So Jeremy wasn't 100 percent positive.

Nonetheless, this small tidbit was all I needed. I turned off my computer, grabbed my coat and left my office early to begin driving the eighty miles up north to Whistler and check out the sighting, to see if it was true.

The sky was liquid with rain – the rainiest day in the world – the thick healthy drizzle that feeds the trees and the ocean and which colors so many of my memories. By 4:00 the sky was already darkening as I passed Horseshoe Bay and began the drive up Highway 99's seaside granite hairpins, up the fjord of Howe Sound, the "Sea to Sky" highway. I was driving slowly; even the headlights had difficulty penetrating the fall of water. Potential chocolate pudding mudslides brooded up the sheer mountain slopes above Montizambert Creek and Lions Bay. In the last light of day at Britannia Beach I was able to see the Pacific Ocean to my left pummeled flat as a sheet of lead.

The richness of the rain made me feel safe and protected; I have always considered the rain to be healing – a blanket – the comfort of a friend. Without at least some rain in any given day, or at least a cloud or two on the horizon, I feel overwhelmed by the information of sunlight and yearn for the vital, muffling gift of falling water.

It was just up past Squamish where I saw the fire – a slag fire from where new land was being cleared – off to the right of the road, past a cluster of brightly lit yellow tractors – a mighty salad of ten thousand stumps and branches – a million tree-rings of time, all burning, all sizzling – a shocking amount of fire, like a lake of fire; so much flame that the rain turned to steam before it hit the embers. I had never seen so much fire in one place at once; I had never believed that there could *be* so much. A field of burning urine and liquid sunsets – I stood in the mud on the sidelines and watched, feeling my skin redden, feeling small cinders singe my skin as the fire calmly raged, like a dream of fire – a fire under the ocean – in the blackness, in the rain, like a secret you just can't keep hidden any longer.

Laurie. This part isn't as straightforward as Walter. Laurie vanished from our family's life five years ago. She was my older sister and for at least a few of the years before she vanished she was closer to me than anybody else, back when we were younger.

My nickname for Laurie was "Louie" and she called me "Louie," too. She was the coolest of all the five kids, the tomboy beauty, the animal lover, the one who had it all together. She was the second born (I am fourth), and it was Laurie who sat on a Donald Duck raft in the pool on a hot summer day, saying she felt like she was floating across Lake Chanel in a giant leather handbag as she made me fetch her Cokes and calcium tablets. She was the one for whom I would skip high school – to go drive around with her in her rusted Ford Courier pickup to smoke bad pot and deliver papers to newspaper boxes, one of her many jobs after high school.

Snapshot: Laurie has borrowed Adam's (my oldest brother's) cordless phone, has dialed it from the kitchen phone, and then stuck the cordless phone in a beehive inside a rotting cedar stump in the backyard forest. The two of us are sitting in the kitchen with our ears to the receiver, listening to the bees buzz.

Another snapshot: in the back yard watching bats dive-bomb a glow-in-the-dark Frisbee we are throwing while waiting for the occasional owl to swoop down from the hemlocks next to the telephone poles, plump and juicy, like a man's head with wings.

Final snapshot: on the afternoon I have obtained my driver's license and have proudly driven in Mom's station wagon down to meet Laurie at another of her jobs, on Marine Drive where she has been dressed as a clown giving out balloons to kids at a franchised fast food place. She has ditched work and has hopped in the wagon with me – dopey wig, makeup and all – and we have cruised around and smoked cigarettes, Laurie having dispensed the finger to those who have incurred our wrath on the road. Afterward we have gone to rummage through Chinatown dumpsters for cool stuff – bamboo slat crates and discarded calendars. Laurie's big foamy clown's feet are sticking out of the debris.

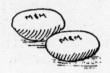

I arrived at Whistler about an hour after I left the fire. Through the rain I saw the clusters of computer generated alpine architecture now lining the roadside, condos mostly, and was surprised at how much the resort had grown from a 1970s ski bum hideaway into its new incarnation as a yuppie hell.

Ski season had not quite begun and the town had the privileged, insider feel of any resort town in the off season: empty roads, buildings with dark windows and closed restaurants. I stopped at the Husky gas station to pick up a map, checked at a pay phone for my phone messages back in Vancouver and then returned to my car. As I did this, two glossy smooth old Karmann Ghias, like M&M's with wheels, pulled up to the pumps from each direction, one red and one yellow.

There was a startled awkward moment as the two drivers noticed the other's car. And then the woman at the cash desk said to me from behind, "Think of what lovely orange babies they'll have." I laughed and for a

191

brief moment I felt I was a part of something larger than just myself, I felt like I had entered a world of magic.

But this is all getting too abstract. Let me talk about real things. Let me talk about when things started to go wrong with Laurie, more than ten years ago, back when I used to believe in the concept of rescuing people.

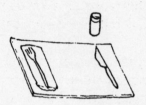

Laurie had always had a mouth on her, and was by far the most argumentative of all the kids – probably the brightest, too. But in her late teens she became, to an alarming degree, alternately sullen, hyperactive and argumentative. She would terrorize the dinner table and all other family gatherings by pointing out to each of us our personality flaws with such insightful precision that we kept our mouths shut for fear she would reveal more. Our get-togethers turned into torment-o-thons.

In retrospect, hers was basic druggie behavior, which matches exactly what other people who have had similar problems with their siblings and children have described to me. But back then it merely seemed as though Laurie was becoming more and more like some of the nastier sides of herself instead of her better ones we knew existed. But we were a family; you may not like another member's development, but you don't question the right of that development to happen.

Laurie always wanted to be Patty Hearst. She would go off into raptures about the kidnapped heiress with me back when I was thirteen and she was seventeen – back when her own major personality changes were beginning. She'd come into my room and say to me with extreme seriousness, "Louie – I want you to imagine something. Sit down. I want you to imagine that you're making a can of Campbell's chicken noodle soup on a weekday night. The TV is playing a *Hawaii Five-O* rerun in the living room. Your hair is a mess and you're in an old terry cloth robe and maybe you're trying to decide if you should make popcorn. The doorbell rings and you shuffle down the hall to answer it. When you do, masked terrorists crash in. They blindfold you and gag you and tie you up and stuff you into the trunk of their Chevrolet. You are whisked away; you are stolen."

I would sit there dutifully through all of this.

"You are taken to your kidnapper's hideaway,

Louie, across the city and locked in a closet and denied proper food and sleep and you are brainwashed with terrorist manifestos. They make you change your name. All links to the past are severed. You disappear from the world completely for months and months."

Laurie always painted a good picture, one of Patty Hearst becoming locked in the world's imagination as a sacrifice to middle-class longing – looted by the forces who would strip our world of tennis shirts and French lessons and gourmet mushrooms: "You are given up for dead, best left in an uninterpreted dream. But then one day you reemerge." (Always with a glint in her eyes.) "You reemerge as a fuzzy black and white image parrying a sawed-off M-1 carbine on the video monitor system of a bank you are robbing in the suburbs of your California hometown." Laurie's lectures tended to end on a similar theme: "You have become a terrorist, an urban guerrilla, cracking the atom of the culture that created you, that you are blinding in a flash of white light."

These lectures sometimes left me terrified and confused. One night, right after one of these diatribes, I caught Laurie purging in the toilet and when I asked her earnestly why she was doing it, she replied, "Just getting my body ready for its new owner."

I think Laurie liked the idea of total transformation that Patty Hearst embodied after she became Tania and began robbing banks for that brief period. I suppose Laurie sensed unstoppable changes happening inside herself and found the Hearst story compatible with those internal changes. Their two lives were not dissimilar, either. Our families were both large and Patty Hearst's hometown was much like ours then – locked in its own dream of outdoor living and high-tech elegance, of stuccoed parabolas and rhodo-dendron flowers and a future full of Plexiglas bubble skylights and ventilated indoor barbecue grills and well-intended concepts for social engineering.

Back up Whistler I continued my drive in the rain, down the highway, wondering, as I neared a possible encounter, exactly what it was I was going to say or do should I actually *find* my sister. I had played out so many possible conversations in my head, both awake and while dreaming over the years, that an actual conversation might be either anticlimactic or might simply feel like another dream. Neither prospect seemed attractive.

Would she smile? Would she be stony-faced? Would she snarl? Would she walk away? Would we touch each other? All these *years* running encounter scenarios over and over in my head, and yet when the possibility of having an encounter really occurred, I had no idea what to say or do.

The Hearst business was only one of Laurie's obsessions. Another was her clothing, which began to get pretty bizarre just after high school – thrift store, but beyond thrift store: random threadbare layers of the ugliest garments – cheesy Polynesian short sleeved shirts of no redeemable beauty matched with olive combat trousers – just crazy stuff; bag lady stuff. And my parents tolerated it, the outfits growing more and more extreme, her body dirtier and dirtier, her behavior more and more outrageous with each successive return home after a failed relationship, a thieving roomie or whatever her reason would be. They put up with it all.

There was nothing in my parents' lives that could have prepared them for Laurie's kind of behavior. Because it was unclassifiable, it went unnoticed and unmentioned. Even after Laurie hit them and stole their money and cracked up the Oldsmobile, or when the RCMP would show up at the door with Laurie bleary-eyed. Never was there any discussion.

I make Laurie sound so horrible here. And I guess I make myself come across as so virtuous – but neither of these is the case. The fact of the matter is that she was simply that much older than me, so she always had an air of unattainable glamour about her. Those few years would always make her seem unknowable to me.

Here's why Laurie pulled away from me in particular: one day we were sitting in the TV room watching some show about psychics. Laurie was maybe twenty and was being like her old self again. If she was nice for even half an hour, we were always, as a family, willing to believe that the old Laurie was back and that everything would be fine again. Suckers.

Anyway, Laurie turned to me and said, "Louie, try being psychic. Guess what I'm thinking about." And I looked at her and didn't even blink an eye – the answer just flashed into my head – it was the name of Peter Zzyzzy, the guy who had always been listed as the last person in the Vancouver telephone book. "Peter Zzyzzy," I said.

Laurie went nuts. She started screaming at me, "How did you know that? How did you *know* that? – *Tell* me!" But of course, I had no way of knowing how I knew – it was a fluke, a pure fluke, and one I could never ever repeat. But that didn't matter. After that, Laurie was stony-faced with me and we never had a real conversation ever again, and nor did she ever call me Louie. At the time this didn't bug me, because frankly we were all pretty annoyed at that point with Laurie's antics, and I was in my senior year at high school and wouldn't have minded a little attention for myself for a change.

Over the next few years, Laurie began systematically going through all of the family members and her friends, finding some small slight the person had committed, whether real or imagined, then magnifying that slight out of all proportion, then cutting that person off forever. It wasn't too long before everyone had been axed, my mother being the last to go.

And it was shortly after this that she simply . . . faded away. To Seattle? To Phoenix? To Toronto? No big farewell scene. Nothing definitive. Just a fading away five years ago. Dad hired some private detectives, but they never found out much – the closest they ever got was three months behind her on the trail – somewhere in Washington State – so if nothing else, we knew she was at least alive. And since then she has been like the family undead person, never alluded to – erased – as though she never existed. Yet of course her presence is felt – at family dinners and weddings and so forth. But it is especially felt on Christmas morning when her presence floats around the yard outside the windows, mocking, fleeting – above the lawn and inside the forest, little glints and rustles which we all know are her, yet which we dare not mention.

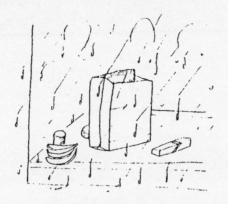

I pulled the car up in front of Nester's grocery store, a few miles past the Whistler Village and got my answer fairly quickly. Even while parked outside I could see what looked to be Laurie inside, putting tins in a customer's bag.

My head went numb. I sat and sat and sat, looking at her form, obscured by rain on the outside of the windows and by steam on the inside.

I saw a phone booth beside the car. I figured I would go look closer through the store's windows. If it was Laurie I would call Brent or my other sister, Wendy, back in town and discuss what to do next. With my arm shaking and my chest shivering, I got out of the car and walked, oblivious to the rain, up to the window and looked inside at the woman at the counter. But it was not Laurie. It was awfully close, but it just wasn't her. I stood for a long time looking at this woman who was not my sister, and then I got back into the car.

I grabbed dinner at an expensive French restaurant that was open in the main Village. I drank a bit of wine and when I came out, the rain was just turning to snow and I left Whistler to return on the winding road back to downtown. The heater in the car had stopped working and it was a miserable drive – cold and boring and slow. I had really been expecting to find Laurie and now that I hadn't, the sense of . . . *unresolvedness* of the situation was immense.

My mind then wandered. I thought of this: I thought of how every day each of us experiences a few little moments that have just a bit more resonance than other moments – we hear a word that sticks in our mind – or maybe we have a small experience that pulls us out of ourselves, if only briefly – we share a hotel elevator with a bride in her veils, say, or a stranger gives us a piece of bread to feed to the mallard ducks in the lagoon; a small child starts a conversation with us in a Dairy Queen – or we have an episode like the one I had with the M&M cars back at the Husky station.

And if we were to collect these small moments in a notebook and save them over a period of months we would see certain trends emerge from our collection – certain voices would emerge that have been trying to speak through us. We would realize that we have been having another life altogether, one we didn't even know was going on inside us. And maybe this *other* life is more important than the one we think of as being real – this clunky day-to-day world of furniture and noise and metal. So just *maybe* it is these small silent moments which are the true story-making events of our lives.

I ramble. I am human; I am trapped inside of time. I just can't believe Laurie's story is over – that it will never end – that I will never know its ending or that there will never be that last little moment that ties it all together. I think of her so often – I wonder if she is happy – or if she is in pain. I wonder what her hair is like nowadays – I wonder what she talks about with new friends she has made – if she has ever been in love or even what she had for lunch. Anything.

I want to tell her that she is kind. I want to tell her that she is good. I want to tell her that God is good, too, and that beauty surrounds us – and that the world is knowable. I want her to come visit me in my house.

Back near Squamish the fire was still burning and the rain was still falling – this rain that will never let up, this fire that will never burn out. The fire so big it makes us forget the rain. I thought of the pioneers that came before me, discovering this world that even now is so new – building railways up into virgin canyons; bridging rivers that flowed from unknown sources; weathering the forest fires, lying motionless in swamps, breathing the smoky air through hollow reeds.

I walked down the road in the rain to a closed gas station and phoned home from the pay phone there. Brent was there. I told him of what had just happened with my failed search for Laurie. I think my voice sounded exhausted, lost and sad.

He told me that he thinks of Laurie all the time, too. He said, "Well at least I have my dreams at night where we can still be friends in the way we used to be. Maybe that's all we're ever going to get. I've learned to try and make myself do with just this."

I agreed. And inside myself I thought about the strange way that dreams provide refuge.

Brent said, "Hey – you're always interpreting your dreams. Here's an idea – why not try something else. Why not interpret your everyday life as though *it* were a dream, instead. Say to yourself, 'A plane's flying overhead now – *What does this mean?*' Say to yourself, 'It's raining so much lately – *What does this mean?*' Say to yourself, 'Today I thought I had rediscovered Laurie – but it turned out it was someone else instead. *What does this mean?*' I think this makes life an easier thing. I really do."

I walked back to the fire, but I got too close and a cinder fell in my hair, burning several strands and giving it the burning hair smell. The odor reminded me of the time when Laurie deliberately burned her eyebrow with a Bic lighter at the dinner table shortly before she left forever.

Memories: I remember watching an old movie once where sleeping gas was sprayed over a city at war. When they woke up, the war was over. Sometimes I think I'll just wake up one morning and Laurie will be normal again, and none of this will have ever happened.

Sometimes, as I have said, I, too, have dreams in which Laurie is whole again and we talk as friends and she makes me laugh. I know, this is only a dream of friendship, not real friendship itself – but it is still lovely.

Already, just two nights ago I had a dream in which Walter the dog was walking inside my house, the nails

209

of his paws clacking snackward, his happy tongue poking out just a little bit from his sweet black face. And last night I had a dream of survival, too – I was floating through the lush forests of the watershed out behind the house I grew up in – through the sky-high trees, floating past all of the plants that grow there, figuring out if I could make it or not if I was left alone in the forest, eating only what foods as are there. And at the end of the dream I emerged into the world of lawns and houses – our house.

Sometimes I'll wonder if Laurie is dead. I think that death is not just dying. I think death is a loss that can never be found again, words that can never be taken back, damage that can never be made whole. It is a denial of any possible future giving of love. Maybe she is dead, but not to me. I really don't think she is.

I began this story talking about the sequencing of life's events, and so I supposed I had best end it with talk of sequence, too. Three episodes from Laurie's life spring to mind, and so I will tell them here. And just because these episodes happened in the past and not in the future – well, it doesn't mean they can't be the end of the story.

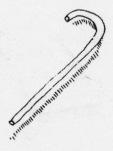

The first incident is this: one of my first memories is of Laurie and me discovering an old woman lost at the corner of Kenwood Road and Southborough Drive. She kept on telling us that she was just at her doctor's office and that she had forgotten her bag of groceries. This confused us because we knew there was nothing except houses and wilderness for many miles in any direction.

We took her home and Mom understood immediately that the old woman was senile and she called the authorities. Laurie sat with the woman on the back patio the whole time and held her hand until the ambulance came and picked the woman up.

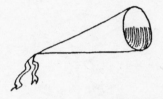

The second incident is this: Laurie once had a favorite story – about a princess who lived in a castle. She used to have me, Brent and Wendy act the story out with her in the forest out back. It went like this – a princess who lived in a castle tower fell in love with a traveling prince from a far off land. Her father the king was furious. He contacted a witch, who made up a forgetting potion for him. The King then went up to his daughter's room in the tower and forced her to drink the witch's potion. He had his guards hold his daughter's arms behind her back while he poured the vile brew down her throat. Once the potion was inside her, the guards let go of her. But then suddenly, before they could stop her, the Princess ran to the window and jumped from the tower to her death, before the potion could take hold of her soul, before she could forget her love.

The last incident is this: Growing up, me, Brent and Laurie would raise Canada geese. Laurie would steal eggs from nests next to the ponds at the golf course; we would incubate the eggs in a tinfoil-lined Johnny Walker whiskey box heated with a 40-watt bulb, turning the eggs over twice each day until they hatched – an event filled with delightful peeping sounds which would continue for the next few blissful months as the peeping graduated into honking.

Geese make wonderful pets – curious, affectionate, loyal and smart as whips. And such fun, too. They would sit beside us on the lawn, picking at the grass while we would read trashy paperbacks and stroke the gentle grey fluff on their chests. Every so often they would crane in with their increasingly longer necks to nibble our ears and give adolescent honking sounds in their insatiable quests for more attention. They were summer friends, waddling behind us around the neighborhood, honking like klaxon horns, hissing at

214

cats and scampering to our sides should we stop for even a moment. During storms they would sit inside perched on the piano stool, afterward scampering back out to the yard and the pond, leaving a trail of lawn-clipping poop in their wake. So much work, but so much fun.

Anyhow, the one thing about Canada geese is that they can only remember you for a year and one day. This is to say that inevitably, no matter how cosmopolitan their upbringing, all geese return to the wild and they forget the family they grew up with; it is a sad truth that colors one's experience with them. But as I have said, they *do* remember you for a year and a day – there is the one day of the year when they come home, just the one time.

Usually it is very early in the morning while you are still deep asleep. You are awakened by a familiar sound, the sound of honking, and so you rush out into the yard with the rest of your family, all of you bleary-eyed. You check the pond and the lawn and find no sign of your old friends. And then you look up on to the roof – up to the roof's crest. There are your old friends, standing on the summit, plump as Thanksgiving turkeys, blaring the happy trumpets that lay rejoicing inside their hearts – letting you know for just this one time, as you stand there waving to them, that their love for you is greater than those forces in the universe that would split apart any of us – that would erase that best part of us – our memories of what once was.

-end-

1,000 YEARS
(LIFE AFTER GOD)

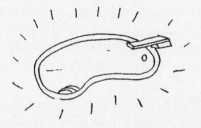

As suburban children we floated at night in swimming pools the temperature of blood; pools the color of Earth as seen from outer space. We would skinny-dip, my friends and me – hip-chick Stacey with her long yellow hair and Malibu Barbie body; Mark, our silent strongman; Kristy, our omni-freckled redheaded joke machine; voice-of-reason Julie, with the "statistically average" body; honey-bronze ski bum, Dana, with his non-existent tan line and suspiciously large amounts of cash, and Todd, the prude, always last to strip, even then peeling off his underwear underneath the water. We would float and be naked – pretending to be embryos, pretending to be fetuses – all of us silent save for the hum of the pool filter. Our minds would be blank and our eyes closed as we floated in warm waters, the distinction between our bodies and our brains reduced to nothing – bathed in chlorine and lit by pure blue lights installed underneath diving boards. Sometimes we would join hands and form a ring like astronauts in space; sometimes when we felt more isolated in our fetal stupor we would bump into each other in the deep end, like twins with whom we didn't even know we shared a womb.

Afterward we toweled off and drove in cars on roads that carved the mountain on which we lived – through the trees, through the subdivisions, from pool to pool, from basement to basement, up Cypress Bowl, down to Park Royal and over the Lions Gate Bridge – the act of endless motion itself a substitute for any larger form of thought. The radio would be turned on, full of love songs and rock music; we believed the rock music but I don't think we believed in the love songs, either then, or now. Ours was a life lived in paradise and thus it rendered any discussion of transcendental ideas pointless. Politics, we supposed, existed elsewhere in a televised non-paradise; death was something similar to recycling.

Life was charmed but without politics or religion. It was the life of children of the children of the pioneers – life after God – a life of earthly salvation on the edge of heaven. Perhaps this is the finest thing to which we may aspire, the life of peace, the blurring between dream life and real life – and yet I find myself speaking these words with a sense of doubt.

I think there was a trade-off somewhere along the line. I think the price we paid for our golden life was an inability to fully believe in love; instead we gained an irony that scorched everything it touched. And I wonder if this irony is the price we paid for the loss of God.

But then I must remind myself we are living creatures – we have religious impulses – we *must* – and yet into what cracks do these impulses flow in a world without religion? It is something I think about every day. Sometimes I think it is the only thing I should be thinking about.

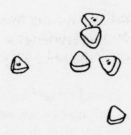

The swimming pools were a decade-and-a-half ago from last July. This was the month in which my doctor had given me a prescription for a certain type of little yellow pill. It is January now.

I had been going through one of life's rough patches – depression and anxiety mostly, and not simply a case of "the blues." It was bigger than that. Nothing cute like a hug or a cluster of silver balloons would cure the moods that had been eating me for the few years prior to then. Dr. Watkin's little triangular lozenges the color of strained-chicken baby food seemed to effectively flatten out my moods – and that was just fine by me.

Dr. Watkin assured me that these pills were extremely common and that most people ended up having to take them at some point in their lives – and I must admit that they did make my temper less haywire. I also became a much "nicer" human being (many of my friends and family had commented on this). As an added bonus, my work became more efficient, and so overall I became a more productive member of society. It was, I suppose, like cosmetic surgery of the brain.

Well, okay, there's more to the pill-thing than this. But maybe you have taken pills in your life, too – and maybe when you took them you didn't know at your deepest levels exactly why you were taking them, only that you were glad that they were there for the taking. That's what it was like with me.

I tell you all of this as I sit here on a forest floor in the wilds of Vancouver Island, inside my old Boy Scout tent, which has been unused for decades. Its plastic ground sheet stinks vaguely of a fridge filled with time-expired yogurt; my hands are clutching my last pack of cigarettes to my chest which is swathed for warmth in my suit jacket and tie and an old grey army blanket. I am trying to keep the cigarettes dry from the rain that leaks inside continuously. Night is falling.

And as you can probably tell, there are things I'm not saying here, things I just can't bring myself to tell you. Please hang on – bear with me – and I will try to tell you more.

Maybe I should tell you about how my fellow fetuses have traveled through life since then – tell you about the odd roads our lives took. And though we took a billion different paths to get where we went, our lives oddly ended up in the same sort of non-place.

First of all, Mark – Mark the strongman, the man who could crush you into petroleum if he wanted to – he tested positive for HIV about two years ago. He's fine enough now – he still works at the brokerage downtown – but for obvious reasons he thinks more about the Last Things than might other people. On rainy nights, we have retro-cocktails (Sidecars, Singapore Slings) at the Sylvia Hotel Lounge, overlooking English Bay.

He looks at his situation in his own way. He will say, "If you really think about it, Scout, our bodies have no way of knowing where they begin and where they end. An immune system doesn't keep you healthy as much as it informs your body where its boundaries lie. Right now it's as if there's this hole that's tunneling through me, confusing my body about where I begin and end – the outside seeping into the inside. Just think of Swiss cheese – if the air holes get too big it stops being a Swiss cheese – it becomes, well . . . *nothing*. I guess that's what I feel is happening to me. I'm becoming nothing. And yeah, it scares me."

Our conversations are never easy, but as I – *we* – get older, we are all finding that our conversations must be spoken. A need burns inside us to share with others what we are feeling. Beyond a certain age, sincerity ceases to feel pornographic. It is as though the coolness that marked our youth is itself a type of retrovirus that can only leave you feeling empty. Full of holes.

On another night at the Sylvia Lounge, with another set of cocktails, Stacey, now a divorced aerobics instructor and paralegal assistant, will say to me, "We were trained to believe our world wasn't magic – simply because it was ours. Why were we taught that magic was something that happened someplace else to other people? Why couldn't they just have told us, 'Kids, this is as good as it gets. So soak it all up while you can'?"

She will finish her second cranberry martini (Crantini). Stacey is an alcoholic now. And her face has that hard look of people who flirt with coke. This saddens me because she is still so beautiful and because I love her more than most of the other people in my life. But I know that the only way she can connect to the "magic" she craves is through the bottle.

As I've gotten older, though, I've learned that there is not much I, or anyone can do in a situation like Stacey's. After a while you can understand the way that things can go wrong in people's lives; you learn all the patterns and the temptations; you recognize the ways people use other people.

The glamour of corruption disappears; the learning is no fun anymore. You don't want to waste the energy, so instead you learn tolerance, and compassion and love – and distance – and these are hard words for me to say. All of this is hard for me to say.

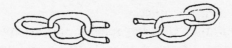

Stacey will become confessional. She will say to me, "There's a big difference between you and me and the rest of the world, Scout," and I will ask her what this is. She will say, "Well you know that point you reach one day – the day where you suddenly crash and realize that you're all alone in the world and you fall into the abyss?"

I will say, "Of course – don't we all?"

Stacey will say, "Well most people are usually living with someone else when that happens and so the expulsion from Eden isn't nearly so bad. But you and me, Scout – we did the mile. We went through the whole shebang alone. We're islands now."

I won't know if this is to be taken as a compliment or not. She will begin to get mushy about Mark, for whom she has always had an unreciprocated longing: "Oh, poor Markie – he's more beautiful than all of us put together and I really think I'd give my own life just so he could stay alive and give the world some scenery for a few more years. Admit it, Scout – you'd give it all away to look like a Chippendale dancer – for even ten *min*utes."

She will realize that her glass is empty and bob her neck in search of the waiter. "And you know *what?* Mark hasn't even told his parents. He thinks they'll a*ban*don him."

Then another Crantini will arrive and I'll know it's soon going to be bailing-out time for me. And then somehow the subject of God will come up. Stacey will look up at me – still so lovely yet so, *so* drunk – and she will say, "Scout, *God* is the teeth of the man who bites me on the back of the neck on a lucky night. *God* is a voice in the night that I hear but I don't worry about because I know who he is. Are you *hear*ing me, Scout?"

"I'm hearing you, Stace," I will say. And I will be listening, too; an earlier version of me would have changed the subject. Somewhere, years ago, so many of us broke the link between love and sex. Once broken, it can never be fixed again.

Julie turned out more "normally" than, say Mark or Stacey. She has two kids and lives in Pemberton Heights in North Vancouver, about as suburban as suburban gets. She has a nice-guy husband, Simon, and looks back upon her earlier years when we were all together as something dangerous and beautiful – but mercifully distant, like the tigers in a pit at a zoo.

"I'm trying to convert my voice these days, Scout," she will tell me as we sit on her front concrete steps drinking weak Mr. Coffee coffee. "You know – I'm trying to escape from ironic hell: cynicism into faith; randomness into clarity; worry into devotion. But it's hard because I try to be sincere about life and then I turn on a TV and I see a game show host and I have to throw up my hands and give up. Too many easy pickin's! Clarity would be so much easier if there weren't so many cheesy celebrities around. Agreed?"

Julie will call out for her two sons to stop fighting with each other over a Super Soaker (as an aside to me she will reveal her code names for them, "Damien" and "Satan") and our talk will continue. "Just ignore the brats."

We will talk some more if it is a warm day and the city before us will glow gold, a dozen construction cranes transforming its profile almost by the hour. She will say, "Thousands of years ago, a person just assumed that life for their kids would be identical to the one that they led. Now you assume that life for the next generation – hell, life next *week* – is going to be shockingly different than life today. When did we start thinking this way? What did we invent? Was it the telephone? The car? Why did this happen? I *know* there's an answer somewhere."

We will talk some more. She will remind me of a night the seven of us had back in 1983. "You know – the night we drank lemon gin and we each stole a flower from the West Van graveyard for our lapels."

I will draw a blank. I won't remember.

"Oh, Scout, don't blank out on me now – you weren't *that* drunk. You gave me all that great advice

233

at that restaurant downtown. I changed *schools* because of that advice."

I will still draw a blank. "Sorry, Julie."

"This is truly pathetic, Scout. *Think*. Markie went shirtless down Denman Street; Todd and Dana and Kristy got fake tattoos."

"Uh – brain death here. Nothing."

Julie will become obsessed with making me remember: "There was that horrible brown vinyl 1970s furniture in the restaurant. You ate a live fish."

"Wait!" I'll cry, "Brown 1970s furniture – I remember brown 1970s furniture."

"Well thank the Lord," Julie will say, "I thought I was going mad."

"No, wait, it's all coming back to me now . . . the flowers . . . the fish." Like a thin strand of dental floss the entire evening will return to me, inch by inch, gently tugged along by Julie. Finally, I will remember the night in its entirety, but the experience will be strangely tiring. The two of us will sit on the warm concrete steps quietly. "What was the point of that story, anyhow?" I will ask.

"I can't remember," Julie will say.

The two of us will be in a bit of shock, me more than Julie, over the nature of memories – of how they're all stored in the brain somewhere, but how they can get lost or simply misfiled or God only knows what. Had Julie not sat there and coached me through the memories of that night, I would have gone to the grave without ever having remembered what was in fact a magical night in my life. And so what would have been the point of having lived that night at all? And so the two of us will be quiet.

It will be time to leave and I will be standing half-inside my car at the end of the driveway by Simon's recently planted baby rhododendrons. Julie will say to me, "Well, so long, James Bond. Back to the bachelor Bat Cave. Wish I could come along with you."

I will think this over and I will say to her, "No you don't. I'd give a million dollars to be able to stay here at this house with *you* – to be Simon for a day."

And she will pause and then she will say, "You know, it's a good life, Scout – but I get lonely here, too – inside the house. Don't fool yourself." She will then give me a peck on the cheek and I will be off, back into the city.

I return to this damp little tent here in the darkening rain forest. It is getting colder now that the daylight behind the overcast rain clouds is gone – but not too cold. It never gets *too* cold here, and this January has been a mild one. The batteries in my flashlight are dead; I didn't prepare for this trip very well – it occurred in somewhat of a hurry – I will explain later. I sit here tugging on a pair of dry, grey, work socks I bought at the PetroCan station in Duncan, while eating my third Kit Kat. The tent now smells somewhat like an Easter egg hunt.

I might as well fill you in on the other three fetuses who shared the swimming pools of my youth. And also, let me tell you this: a week ago, I threw away the pills Doctor Watkin gave me. They now lie buried inside a brown plastic Shoppers Drug Mart vial snug within the municipal landfill. So it's truly the real me you're hearing. Not the pills.

Just to reassure you.

Dana.

Dana was the most experimental of the seven of us. We knew he did all sorts of fringe things, but with us he made an effort to be "normal" (that word again). I suppose that was our attraction to him. It wasn't until years later that I found out just how fringy some of his behavior was.

He took me into his West End apartment, on the twentysomethingth floor of some 1960s concrete tooth, and, in a mood of general confession, showed me a stack of porn mags with Post-it notes stuck inside various pages and said, "Look." I did, and there was Dana at various ages over the years, no tan lines, doing just about everything with just about everybody. I was speechless. What can one say?

He then took me to a cupboard with a vacuum cleaner and a few boxes of Tide. From one of the Tide boxes he removed a clear plastic bag full of something that was not Tide. From there we walked into the bathroom and he flushed away the equivalent of an Ivy League education for a set of twins.

We then went into his living room – IKEA furniture and yuppie electronic toys covered with cigarette burns, smoked one last cigarette and looked at the sun shining silver over the sailboats in English Bay. "I just wanted a witness, that's all," he said.

"Then I'm your witness," I replied.

"I've changed," he said.

"I'm glad," I said.

There was silence then some awkward good-byes and then I let myself out of the apartment, and it was years before I saw Dana again. It was in the parking lot of the Save-On-Foods supermarket at the Park & Tilford shopping mall. He was loading a mini-van with groceries while a woman strapped a baby into a child safety seat while trying to discipline an older, noisier child beside it.

I walked up to him and said, "Dana! Long time, no see."

Fear was in his eyes. The woman – his wife – looked up curiously, and Dana hastily introduced me as Scout: "We used to play football together in high school."

"Isn't that nice," she said, and continued strapping in the child.

"Hey look, you've got kids –" I said, "great. When did you get married?"

Dana cut me short. He slammed the rear door,

shoved away the shopping cart without bothering to get his 25 cents back from the cart's lock device, fumbled with his keys and headed to the driver's door. "I can't talk to you, Scout. I just can't."

"Hey – okay, okay. No probs, man," I said.

Dana turned the ignition. His wife smiled and waved at me and shouted "Nice to meet you!" through the decreasing crack in the window that Dana was rolling up.

A week later, around six at night, Dana phoned me up – I'm not hard to reach: my phone number has been the same for almost ten years – and he was obviously at a pay phone, with cars and trucks roaring in the background.

"It's me," he said.

"I figured. You okay?"

A pause. "Absolutely."

I tried to make conversation and felt vaguely like I was in a quiet room with somebody on terminal life support. "Your wife seems nice," I said.

"I pray for you," he replied.

"Oh," I said. "Uh – thanks."

"I pray for you because you have no faith and hence no soul."

"Hey, Danester – I may be faithless, but I'm not without a soul. I'll thank you not to patronize me, either."

"God is descending into the suburbs, Scout. We

240

never expected judgement in our time, but it is going to happen."

"Dana? What's the deal?"

"The time is coming, Scout. You will not have to live inside linear time anymore; the concept of infinity will cease to be frightening. All secrets will be revealed. There will be great destruction; structures like skyscrapers and multinational corporations will crumble. Your dream life and your real life will fuse. There will be music. Before you turn immaterial, your body will turn itself inside out and fall to the ground and cook like steak on a cheap hibachi and you will be released and you will be judged."

"Um – Dana . . . I think I have somebody on call waiting. Can I phone you back?"

"You may be driving in a car when it happens. You may be shopping in a fashionable store. You may be . . ."

"Hey Dana. Gotta go. *Ciao*."

And there is Dana.

Todd's life has changed the least of any of us. He dropped out of Simon Fraser University over a decade ago and began scamming full-time between tree planting and unemployment insurance – a way of life he shows no signs of ever altering. He shares a 1940s house off Commercial Drive in East Vancouver with an ever-changing ragtag ensemble of ecofreaks, slackers, Deadheads, Québecois nationalists, mountain bikers and part-time musicians.

Our biggest common bond is that right after high school we spent two summers together tree planting, gypsying about from contract to contract, sowing seedlings in clearcuts spanning British Columbia – Bowron Lake, Camper Creek, the Okanagan, Nelson, Tzenzaicut, the Sheemahant Valley. We had herbicide dumped in our faces from upwind helicopters; we swam in cranberry bogs; we heard strangers tap on motel windows up in the Queen Charlotte Islands whispering *"hash . . . 'shrooms . . . coke . . ."*; we took thirty-minute group showers in Prince George, sharing precious hot water and scraping off charcoal from clearcut burns with pumice blocks. It was a good time of life; Todd never left it.

I will visit Todd's house and he will tell me his theories about literally everything. I visit him only a few times a year – he never visits me downtown. He will sit perched on his Balans chair, the pads of which are covered with Dr. Seuss's *The Lorax* T-shirts, while he eats a sublingual B-12 vitamin.

"Hi, Todd," I will say above a full-volume Fortran 5 tape that will be acting as a soundtrack to a muted zombie film on the VCR.

"Dudeski, Dudeski, *Dudeski* – snack?" He will offer me something lumpy that rests in an abalone shell, and I will say, "Sure," and he will toss a sourdough bun to me across the braid-rugged floor strewn with wine skins, foam pads, cargo pants, sleeping bags, wool socks, a surfboard, kitty squeak toys and jumbo Tiki salad forks and spoons.

Todd will be dressed in biking shorts, fingerless wool gloves, and an Aran sweater from Value Village. Soggy Cowichan sweaters will line the hooks in the front hallway. I will feel hopelessly bourgeois in whatever I am wearing, and sit in the surplus Boeing 737 seat near Todd's Balans chair.

"Todd," I will say, "can I turn down the music?"

"Huh? What's that?"

I will turn off the music; there will be peace and then we will talk.

"Treeplanting pays spittle," he will say. I won't bother pointing out he *does* have other options in life.

Todd will be restless. Perhaps he will be on some sort of drug. Stacey ended up alcoholic but Todd ended up the druggie. Mark calls Todd's lifestyle "wake n' bake."

Todd will fiddle with the buttons of a Motorola walkie-talkie lying on top of a stack of Macintosh diskettes. Outside, teenagers drag-race on nearby Commercial Drive. Performance artists agitated by too many espressos screech the *Jeopardy!* theme song like randy tomcats. There is the feeling of colorful, snug chaos. Chaos with an undercurrent of disturbing randomness.

We will talk about the old times a bit, but Todd won't be much interested. I'm the only one of the old group he keeps up with, and even then, it's entirely through my own efforts. The possibility of a reunion for all seven of us is pretty much out of the question.

But then, every so often, through the fog of drugs and a downwardly spiraling lifestyle, the real Todd will shine through, and then I remember why I make the effort to see him through the years. For example, I will ask him what he thinks about while he plants baby trees in the lobotomized northern clearcuts. He will snarl and laugh (his dental work – oh!) and say, "The money, Dudeski, the money," and then he will stop and say, "You not that's not true. Man you *know* that was just a bad joke. Do you really want to know what I think about when I'm out there?"

"Yes."

"I think about this . . . I think about how hard it is – even with the desire, and even with the will and the time – I think of how hard it is to reach that spot inside us that remains pure that we never manage to touch but which we know exists – and I try to touch that spot."

He will place a pinch of Drum tobacco on a rollie

and he will squint. "Man, what else is there? I've never touched that spot yet, but I'm still trying."

He will light his cigarette and reflect. He will then reach for me in my surplus 737 seat, grab me by one shoulder and place his other hand on top of my head, and then seemingly yank my spirit out of my body through the top of my skull with a great pull, shocking me.

He will then say, looking at my body, "Here you are. You have this meat thing here – your *corpse* – and then here you have . . ." he will look at my imaginary spirit, draped from the fingers of his other hand, *"You."*

I will feel dizzy. I will feel as though Todd has cut me in two.

"What is *you*, Scout? What is the *you* of *you*? What is the link? Where do *you* begin and end? This *you* thing – is it an invisible silk woven from your memories? Is it a spirit? Is it electric? What exactly *is* it?"

He will gently, mime-like, place my spirit back into my body and I will be glad.

He will pat me on the head. "Don't sweat it, man. You're all there. Nothing escaped."

We will sit and listen to the silence for a while. Then Todd will speak some more. He will say, "Oh, I know you guys think my life is some big joke – that it's going nowhere. But I'm happy. And it's not like I'm lost or anything. We're all too fucking middle class to ever be lost. Lost means you had faith or something to begin with and the middle class never really had any of that. So we can never be lost. And you tell *me*, Scout – what is it we end up being, then – what exactly *is* it we end up being then – instead of being lost?"

Finally: Kristy. I work with her every day out at the software company – a shiny emerald box in an industrial park in Richmond on the delta flatlands off of Highway 99. She's in marketing and I'm in sales, so we "interact" a good deal on a business as well as a personal level, speaking a complex body language of mockery and suppressed giggles across the room during general meetings. We goof off whenever we can.

At the moment Kristy is having "a mad pash" with the owner of the company, Bryce. This has been going on for at least half a year. And even though the company itself is one enormous gossip generator, no one knows about it except me. The thing with Kristy is that she can only fall for men she thinks are smarter than herself – a factor that ruled out Todd, Dana, Mark and me a long time ago. A factor that rules out most guys. Bryce is a software egghead, so I guess that puts him on a higher plane.

"And he's married, too," Kristy will add over gin

and tonics at the local sports club during lunch hour, a locale awash in the smell of limes, terry towels and highly advertised men's colognes. "That makes him doubly attractive." Kristy, it should be noted, equates marriage with intelligence even though she, herself, has a hard time seeing herself in a veil.

One of Kristy's bigger worries is that she'll continue her pattern of desiring only the unattainable and then one day, well, in her own words: "My ability to fall in love for real will just sort of atrophy and then I'll replace my capacity for love with sentimentality – you know – knitting bibs for my sister's kids; sobbing over puppies; going overboard at Christmas and wearing red and green dresses; vanity mirrors surrounded by inspirational decoupage plaques. Should this ever happen, Scout, please, *please* telephone the Symbionese Liberation Army and have them come and kidnap me."

Anyway, Kristy figures again in this story, so I will come back to her. But for now I think it best to describe how I ended up here in this tent, dressed in a suit and tie, in the forest. And maybe I should talk a bit about myself – something I have been avoiding until now.

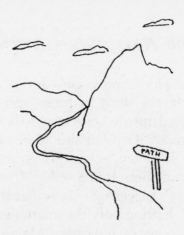

Some facts about me: I think I am a broken person. I seriously question the road my life has taken and I endlessly rehash the compromises I have made in my life. I have an unsecure and vaguely crappy job with an amoral corporation so that I don't have to worry about money. I put up with halfway relationships so as not to have to worry about loneliness. I have lost the ability to recapture the purer feelings of my younger years in exchange for a streamlined narrow-mindedness that I assumed would propel me to "the top." What a joke.

Compromise is said to be the way of the world and yet I find myself feeling sick trying to accept what it has done to me: the little yellow pills, the lost sleep. But I don't think this is anything new in the world.

This is not to say my life is bad. I know it isn't . . . but my life is not what I expected it might have been when I was younger. Maybe you yourself deal with this issue better than me. Maybe you have been lucky enough to never have inner voices question you about

250

your own path – or maybe you answered the questioning and came out on the other side. I don't feel sorry for myself in any way. I am merely coming to grips with what I know the world is truly like.

Other thoughts: sometimes I wonder if it is too late to feel the same things that other people seem to be feeling. Sometimes I want to go up to people and say to them, "What is it you are feeling that I am not? *Please* – that's all I want to know."

Perhaps you think I simply need to fall in love and that maybe I've just never met the right person. Or perhaps I've just never figured out exactly what it was I wanted to do with life while the clock ticked away. Whatever.

Like most people, I've bottomed out a few times; in motel rooms, say – alongside naked bodies close by in cities I can't recall – looking at phones with nobody to dial. And I've been hooked on a few things, too, and lost months and years there, but I think I came out of it with my brain cells intact. And how much would this matter, anyway?

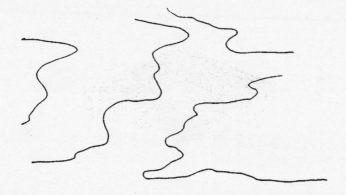

Sometimes I want to go to sleep and merge with the foggy world of dreams and not return to this, our real world. Sometimes I look back on my life and am surprised at the lack of kind things I have done. Sometimes I just feel that there must be another road that can be walked – away from this person I became – either against my will or by default.

But then I think about this: during family dinners, Mom and Dad used to talk about how they met each other – of how Mom changed her usual path to the library one day and saw Dad, and they smiled and made the first connection. It is a sweet story, and one we never tired of hearing over and over again, savoring the repetitive details of their creation myth: the dress she was wearing, the books they were carrying, their first soda. The story was always bookended by my father saying, "Just think, kids – if your mother had taken her usual route to the library, none of you would be here today!"

I have thought my father's statement over many times, and his idea seems absurd. I know in my bones that I would have made it here anyway – somehow. I have this funny feeling that I wouldn't have missed Earth for anything. So I must be getting *some*thing out of the experience.

Anyway, here's how I wound up inside this tent in the dark and rain on the west coast of Vancouver Island: last week I went to New York on a business trip along with two other guys from the company, Cameron and Shiraz. I was still taking the little yellow pills then.

It was not a glamorous trip – no cocktails with Angie Dickinson astride the Chrysler building's eagles or anything like that – merely endless meetings and fear; hierarchy-addicted weasels and dinners with drunk product reps. There was a hysteria-packed motivational seminar and in between all this, furtive scurryings with Cameron to Eighth Avenue pornography dens. The company's travel agent had located the tiniest, cheapest hotel rooms in Manhattan and they smelled like basements. The unending grumble of traffic down below interrupted what little sleep I could grab. A salesman's life.

It was also the January of the presidential inauguration; much of the news that weekend dwelt on the ceremonies to occur down in Washington on the following Wednesday, and for some reason I had been paying more attention to this news than I might have otherwise. I don't consider myself political; being Canadian, American politics have only a detached appeal. Yet there I was, lying on my hotel room's musty bed sheet, umpteen rotations of CNN news into the night, sirens flaring on the streets below, wondering about the transition of power about to occur in the city to the South.

I was wondering what the ceremony itself would be like – it was like wondering about a coronation – of the old king being dead – long live the new king. I was wondering about trumpeters raising their horns, of the crowds – of the world somehow becoming new again in the process. I was thinking and feeling this through the mist of my doctor's yellow pills. I figured the inauguration must have meant something important to me to cut through the fog.

It was on Tuesday morning that I was scheduled to grab a cab to LaGuardia for my return flight to Vancouver. Instead, however, I surprised even myself and walked the ten blocks to the Penn Station Amtrak counter where I paid for tickets and caught the Metroliner for Washington, DC. I rationalized that it was my one chance in life to see a spectacle like an inauguration; I don't think I thought of it on any other level.

From a phone on the train I called an old college friend of my brother's, Allan, who works at World Bank – a loner type whose old UBS dorm room had once been a museum of *Star Trek* paraphernalia. Allen said he would be glad to have me visit, and to my surprise he was even having company over that evening. Allan also invited me to crash on his living room floor for the night if I wanted, and I realized that I hadn't even thought of what I would have done had he not asked me.

I arrived. Allan lived in a third-floor apartment on Capitol Hill, behind the Capitol building, and his *Star Trek* geekery of yesteryear had merely been upgraded to the newer *Trek* generations. Allan's friends showed up around 7:30 and turned out to be his Dungeons & Dragons gaming cohorts. They spent the evening discussing skulls and levels and kings and spells and charms and swords and warlocks. "Beverages" proved to be tap water, Jell-O powder and gin.

I have to admit, the evening was fun – I was a stranger in a strange city among friendly people. It was as though my past life no longer existed – that other life where I theoretically should have been in a jet eight miles above Idaho, headed to Vancouver and the life I was losing my ability to understand.

I felt as if I was living a stranger's life. I was beginning to feel like a person inside a story for the first time in years. I almost didn't want to sleep that night, not wanting that feeling to vanish. In fact, I felt so different that for the first night in months I decided not to take my little yellow pills.

I slept soundly – and all through the night, the concentration of yellow pills in my blood diminished, milligram by milligram, like decaying uranium.

The next morning, the morning of the inauguration, I was sitting on Allan's wobbly hardwood floor, with the sun streaming through the windows on to a Siamese cat that lay cradled in my lap. The sun picked up motes of dander as I scratched its chest. Allan and I watched the actual swearing-in ceremony on CNN. The cat hopped out of my lap, arched its back and then propped itself up against the windowsill, looking out the window at the day.

The streets outside the window in our part of the city were silent, whereas the afternoon before there had been the grind of practicing school choirs from Illinois, satellite linkup trucks, secret service men buzzing each other, joggers and barking dogs. Now all of the action was on the other side of the Capitol building.

After the swearing-in ceremony was finished on CNN, we walked down on to the street to see if we could see the old president's helicopter leaving the Capitol building – and we could. Other people from houses along the street were doing the same thing, and we all stood there under the warm January sun on a street with no cars, watching the helicopter rise, hover and depart, like a science fiction creature. As I went back into the apartment I looked at the yards in front of the houses: frost had not done much damage that year and the soil of the city sprouted with narcissi and chives and dandelion.

I then got dressed in a shirt and tie and walked down to Pennsylvania Avenue where the citizens stood ten-deep waiting for the parade. It was sweater weather and the people of the city were in high spirits. Junkies the color of vanilla milk shakes wore their finest baseball caps; florally upholstered Mary Kay queens ate bagels sold from street vendors. The suburban folk who had ventured into the city wore down vests and ski jackets; some of the older folks wore tweed coats and dashing hats. Everywhere there was a sense that today did not have to be like other days; there was a sense that just for one day, the city was open to everyone and free of danger. And the roar they made! The noise! the clapping – the cheering! It was so loud, a deafening beauty.

I squished myself into the crowd in front of the Canadian Embassy, 501 Pennsylvania Avenue, just as the parade began. Secret service people lurked everywhere as the big moment came when the President himself passed by us. As he did, a boys' varsity basketball team from Rockville, Maryland, lifted an old woman in her wheelchair up high so that she could see him, and the clapping became ecstatic. After the President had passed, a piping band marched by and the music made my eyes water. I remembered there was a war going on and the music was a reminder of the beauty that often accompanies destruction.

And then suddenly I realized that I was feeling – well, that I was actually *feeling*. My old personality was, after months of pills and pleasant nothingness, returning. Just the littlest bit – for I had only stopped taking my little yellow pills the day before – but my essence was already asserting itself, however weakly at this point. I felt a lump in my throat, and I spent the rest of the day walking around this strange and beautiful city, remembering myself, what it used to feel like to be me, before I switched myself off, before I stopped listening to my inner voices.

This process continued into the night. I ate dinner at a Burger King. Allan was asleep by the time I shuffled in, exhausted. And all through the next day's flight back home, more and more of myself trickled back into the vessel of my body, drop by drop by drop as the jet flow over Idaho, back home from my brief interlude in the radically different world of the East.

The next night at 9:30 I was back in Vancouver, in my apartment in Kitsilano, a scenic, hilly, Jeep-clogged beer commercial of a neighborhood over-looking the ocean. I walked through the door, phoned in sick to the office, unplugged my phone, drew the shades, locked the doors and went to bed. Over the next week I emerged only to visit the corner hippie food store to buy textured tofu, veggies, loganberry juice and soy milk.

Memories ran through my head this week, memories of photos I had once seen of houses drowned by floods in northern British Columbia during the great hydroelectric projects of the 1960s. Decades later, when the water levels dropped, these ghostly houses would reappear amid mud flats and flopping, asphyxiating fish. I felt myself now walking through one of these strange houses, now *my* house, putting pictures up on the greyed, mired wood, putting thick Persian rugs on the snaggletoothed floor, painting the warped walls bright colors – relighting the fireplace that had been at the bottom of the sea for so long.

I never expected to become this strange person I had become, but I was determined to know who this person was.

And so I sat, bunkered away for a week, coming off the pills, thinking and dreaming alone – as do we all, I suppose.

It was only this morning, Wednesday morning – a week since the inauguration – that I drove down to my old office, down at the industrial park in Richmond off Highway 99, stopping first for some doughnuts at the Lansdowne Mall, savoring their sugary burst of artificiality after a week of hippie food.

I only got as far as my office's parking lot, though, beside its unadorned aquamarine glass box when I froze in my car, three parking aisles back. I was feeling sick to my stomach, unable to get out. I was dressed for work today – I had thought I would be able to do it – but in the end I couldn't bring myself to leave the car, to enter the building.

After maybe half an hour or so, Kristy came out of the main entrance of the building, carrying two Styrofoam cups of coffee and got in the car and sat in the passenger seat. She asked me what was new and I said, "Oh, you know – life, I guess."

And she asked, "Growing a beard?"

I said, "Uh, yeah."

After a guilty pause she asked, "Ummm, Scout – you're not planning on randomly sniping us miserable employees here, are you?"

I said, "No – not this week."

"No senseless blood bath? No carnage?"

"Sorry."

"Well then, that's a relief." She checked her makeup in the vanity mirror underneath the passenger seat visor. "Everybody's been looking at you through the windows wondering if you had a Uzi in the trunk. Feeling not-sick anymore?"

"Not as much."

"Good."

We sat drinking the coffee and looking at the building. The glass was one-way, so we couldn't see inside, but we could see the clouds reflected in the glass: bumper car clouds – the puffy type in which you can easily imagine animal shapes.

I asked Kristy what was new in the office and she said that R&D was releasing a project for a memory system called "Flavor Crystals" in which memory was stored "in buds, like in Tang or something. I'm not quite sure I understand."

I was silent and our little sips of coffee from the Styrofoam were depressing. Kristy said to me, "You know, Scout, I think it's time for one of our therapy cruises. Don't you?"

LIFE AFTER GOD

    I agreed. I started the car, reversed out of the lot, and then pulled riverward, out through the agricultural flatlands.

The two of us held our hot beverages, driving the speed limit while looking at the bleak January blueberry and strawberry farms and the falling-apart old barns. It felt good to be moving. It felt good to not be near the office. It felt good to be with Kristy.

The tide was out and we stopped the car to look for drift-stuff. We were at the spot where the Fraser River meets the ocean and the river turns to salt. There were sticks and bits of plastic and old logs and pieces of old plywood and bits of broken boats and wooden doors. Piles and piles of this debris went on for as far as we could see.

I guess the barns and this old jetsam made Kristy think of aging. She asked, "Is it me, Scout, or is time going all weird for you, too?"

"How so?" I was poking a stick at an old window frame.

"I mean, does a day still feel like a day to you, or

269

does it just *zing* right by? Is time passing too quickly for you, too?"

"I think so. I think it's the spirit of the age. All these machines we have now. Like phone answering machines and VCRs. Time collapses."

"I used to think time was like a river," she said, hopscotching from log to log, "that it always flowed at the same speed no matter what. But now I think that time has floods, too. Or that it just simply isn't a constant any more. I feel like I'm in the flood."

I said that time was linked to emotions. "Maybe the more emotions a person experiences in their daily lives, the longer time seems to feel to them. As you get older, you experience fewer new things, and so time seems to go by faster."

"Christ, how depressing," said Kristy.

We walked and poked amid the silver-grey field of drift-things. Kristy asked me, "Scout, do you ever think sometimes that maybe you're a bit *past* love?"

"Me?"

"No – *me*, I mean. I wonder if I'm turning into an old hosebag."

I threw a stick to an imaginary dog. "I doubt it. From what I can see, love is always lurking around the corner. Maybe you'll be one of those women who fall for a jailed serial killer."

"Thanks."

This was one of those conversations where you looked at the scenery, not each other. I said, "Yeah, I *do* worry if I'm past love – or if that capacity was even there in the first place."

"I woke really early this morning," said Kristy, "and I thought to myself – 'So, girl – this is *it*? Forty more years of *this*? Something's got to change, girl. Some-

271

thing's got to change.' And it's true. Something does. I need something. Or maybe I need to throw something away. But something has to change now. I can't go on like this any longer."

"Did you fall out of love with Bryce?" I asked.

"Not yet. But it'll happen soon enough, that moment where The Other turns into a tacky stranger and I can't believe what a loser I was to hook up with him in the first place."

"Gee, that's certainly an optimistic point of view."

"But it's true. As I age I find I'm simply unwilling to pursue any relationship that I know from the start is just not going to work – what sort of callous old broad am I?"

"An efficient old broad?" I ventured.

We walked further on, then – a confession from Kristy: "My big fear is getting married and falling out of love."

"Big Surprise, Kris. That's *every*body's big fear. Everybody's. But most people pass through it." I was surprised that Kristy should confess to me a fear which, from her lips, seemed almost naïve.

We walked further, watching the birds peck amid the wood bits, just as we pecked amid them, too. Kristy asked, "Aren't you worried about just *making do* in life?"

"Sure."

"How do you deal with it?"

"Until recently I don't think I *have* been dealing with it."

There was a pause and then Kristy turned to me, smiling: "You weren't sick last week, *were* you, Scout?"

"Technically, no."

"Where were you?"

"At home. Just thinking."

"Polishing your rifles? Muttering to yourself about conspiracy theories?"

"No. Just thinking. You know, I went to Washington after New York. To see the inauguration ceremonies."

"See any celebs?"

"No."

"Meet the prez?"

"No."

"Why'd you go?"

"I'm not sure. But there was something there I needed to see – evidence of a person or a thing larger than a human being."

"And . . .?"

"And . . . I came home and ended up spending the week bunkered away – *thinking*."

I knew that Kristy was dying to know what conclusions I had made, but I am ashamed to say that I was too embarrassed to tell her. Instead I changed the subject. "Did I ever tell you," I said, "about the time

273

last year in Stanley Park when Mark and I went rollerblading?"

"No."

"There was this group of blind people, with white canes and everything – a C.N.I.B. tour or something – and they heard us coming, and they motioned for us to stop, and we did. Then they handed Mark a camera. They asked Mark to take their picture."

"Blind people?"

"Exactly. But the strange thing was, they still believed in sight. In pictures. I'm thinking that's not a bad attitude."

It was nice being with Kristy like this, just hanging out. It reminded me of the old days, of being fetal in the swimming pools. I mentioned to her one of my favorite fantasies: to be in a coma for one year and wake up and have a whole year's backlog worth of news to catch up on.

"Me too!" she cried. "Fifty-two whole issues of *People* to catch up on – it'd be like *heroin* – information overdosing."

We got back into the car, and Kristy was still in her *People* magazine mode. She asked me, "Do you ever wonder who it is who people will remember in a thousand years – and, I mean – do you think they'll get it *right*? I mean, *'There was once the Great Madonna and She was so fabulous that She lived on the 500th floor of the Empire State Building and consumed 1,000 Pepsis every day.'* Stuff like that."

I said we'll probably remember Einstein, Marilyn Monroe and that's it. And then I changed my mind. I said, "You know what people will probably think of when they think of these days a thousand years from now? They'll look back upon them with awe and wonder. They'll think of Stacey – or someone like Stacey – driving her convertible down the freeway, her hair flowing back in the wind. She'll be wearing a bikini and she'll be eating a birth control pill – and she'll be on her way to buy real estate. *That's* what I think people will remember about these times. The freedom. That there was a beautiful dream of freedom that propelled the life we lived."

"It seems impossible to imagine a thousand years," said Kristy. "I think that one lifetime is all the time human beings are capable of imagining."

"You're probably right. I think as humans we're only allowed certain viewpoints about time. And they're probably not the correct ones, either. Time is probably something else altogether. So I wouldn't panic about it."

"You *have* been bunkered away for a week, haven't you?"

"We'd probably best be driving you back to the Evil Empire," I said.

Minutes later we pulled back into the parking lot. Kristy put her Styrofoam cup, scarred with fingernail indents and lipstick bruises, on to the dashboard's top. "I take it you're not coming back in," she said.

"No. Probably not," I said.

"Any particular reason?"

"That kooky bunkering, you know. It makes you see life differently."

"Can I come over and visit you sometime soon?"

"Always."

Bryce's Porsche pulled into the lot. Kristy looked at it. "Guess I'd best be going." She kissed me on the lips. "You know, I think I'm beginning to think you're smarter than I am."

"We'll talk soon."

She skipped back into the office.

But the forest – the forest . . . *how* did I end up in this rain soaked tent in the middle of nowhere?

I have told you part of the story. But there is a little bit more. It happened like this: Decades ago, my father would take my brothers and sisters and me on fishing trips into northern British Columbia. This was back when we were all young enough that our daily experiences were converting from dreams into memories – permanent memories.

I dreaded these trips, regarding them, as the youngest of many children often do, as merely a new mode in which my elder siblings might creatively format their tormentings of myself.

Needless to say, my siblings loved these journeys, deep, deep into the worlds of Nowhere – far from the comfort of television and the mall and hot food. British Columbia was far more primitive then, even a short time ago, in the 1960s.

Now, decades later, the torments, whatever they

were, are long forgotten. But what remains in my head are the memories of the landscapes we entered as a family: the raw mountains; the charging rivers; the purity of it all. What also remains is my unshakable sense that the undiscovered world is indeed larger than the world we think we know.

And so, after returning home to Kitsilano and staring at my stale apartment and hearing the mumbles of traffic outside, it was these memories of these landscapes that made me choose to retreat further into myself, to head into the wilderness.

As long as there is wilderness, I know there is a larger part of myself that I can always visit, vast tracts of territory lying dormant, craving exploration and providing sanctity.

And so *that* is how I ended up here in the forest tonight, in this soaking wet tent – impulse, sheer mad impulse, and – given my current level of discomfort – bad planning. But it's okay.

And here's how I left the city: I rifled through the front hall closet and the kitchen and began stuffing things into an old blue duffel sport bag – sweat clothes, baseball caps, a box of Ritz crackers, hiking boots, a flashlight. . . . I tossed the bag into the rear seats of my ancient Volvo along with my old Boy Scout tent, and simply departed, off for the Vancouver Island ferry at Horseshoe Bay over in West Vancouver.

My old car rumbled through downtown, over road ramps that twisted like proteins, through a fishy smelling breeze, past skyscrapers, past a CBC TV tower, past totem poles and jet-lagged Japanese tourists forlornly roaming the sidewalks. Then over Lions Gate Bridge and over Burrard Inlet where mallard ducks sleep in the cold water currents along the black and white spines of killer whales.

The ferry was just loading at Horseshoe Bay, and I slid right on, and for the 90-minute trip to Vancouver Island, I watched the puffs of cloud in the sky degenerate into serious rain weather.

Disembarking off the clanking ferry ramp at Nanaimo, I drove the Trans-Canada highway south and then turned Pacific Oceanward at Duncan, off toward Lake Cowichan and the pulp mill town of Youbou. There, the road turned to dirt and the potholes were filled with milky bruises of rainwater. A ghostly procession of ecological activists in yellow and green rain slickers marched down the road, like a conscience.

I drove for two hours, not seeing any other cars or logging trucks, but sometimes I would hear the logging trucks changing gears on the other side of a mountain, like a dinosaur's howl. The sides of the road were strewn, like bones, with loggers' debris – coffee cups, grease-gun cartridges, rags, steel cables and spray-paint cans. Gravel ripped at my car's under panels; I crossed a river of shocking liquid emerald; I headed upward and inward into the mountains and their mists.

I drove along the logging roads with the windows open, with bracing winds and splashes of rain pelting inside – along winding hairpinning roads, through clearcuts, through ancient rain forests, through tree farms, careful all the while to look for washouts on the road and for fallen snags.

I felt like an old person with Alzheimer's, who gets into their car to drive to the corner store, and then forgets what they were looking for and is found driving days later, thousands of miles away.

After another hour of this I saw a logging company's road-numbering sign: HADDON 1,000. This magic number was the only clue I needed to know that I was where I wanted to be.

I followed a short road down a hill that ended in a cul-de-sac. This cul-de-sac was beside an ancient, unharvested rain forest. If I had once thought of life as an endless car ride, then now my car had finally stopped.

I thought this: I thought of how an embryo doesn't know where on Earth or when in history it is going to be born. It simply pops out of its womb and joins its world. The landscape I saw before me is the world that I had joined, the world that made me who I am.

And with this in mind, I stepped out of the car.

It was late afternoon as I popped the trunk and reached for the duffel bag. I took a green Glad garbage bag from next to the spare tire, ripped a hole in its bottom, and placed it over top of my suit, poking other holes out for my arms. I removed my office shoes and put on my hiking boots and stuck a small black toque over my head. Then, carrying my duffel bag with one arm and my tent with the other, I walked into the deep green forest, my feet silent on the shaggy moss.

The sky was breathless, with no sounds of engines, no sounds of jets. All surfaces around me burst with life, with liverworts and tongues of ferns and shiny green coins of salal.

I saw massive Douglas firs that had fallen long ago – whales of biomass – the sky made solid – millennia worth of nutrients inhaled from the heavens now feeding bracket fungi and nursing rows of baby firs along their lengths. I tried to count one tree's rings but gave up back near the Dark Ages, before I could reach the Roman Empire or the birth of Jesus.

The undergrowth was lush and moist. Fuzzy dendrites of pale green Old Man's Beard moss brushed my cheeks. I walked deeper and deeper into this organism, this brain, imagining man-made noises where I knew none could be, finding it hard to believe that true silence could exist.

After an hour's walk into the forest, I pitched my tent, under a juggernaut spruce tree, its bark like a dimpled, dark grey shark-skin. A stream flowed below me, running clear, running fresh. And so I made my tent and crawled in as the sky began to darken, preparing my story, preparing to join the world of trees and their massively parallel sleep.

283

And that is my story until now. Here I now lie, on my stomach, looking out at the dark wet world, pulling the blanket tighter around me, smoking a cigarette, and knowing that this is the end of some aspect of my life, but also a beginning – the beginning of some unknown secret that will reveal itself to me soon. All I need do is ask and pray.

I stub out my cigarette, close the tent flaps, and lay back on the ground sheet on top of the soil. I close my eyes and prepare to sleep, but something underneath me nudges my spine.

I reach my arms out of the flaps, into the rain, and underneath the ground sheet, where I pluck out a small object. I bring it back inside and feel it – it is a spruce pine-cone. I smell it, cold and wet, and then hold it up to my cheek. I then stick my arm back outside the tent and plant the cone into the soil, just below the ground sheet.

1,000 Years (Life After God)

Time is how the trees grow. I will fall asleep for a thousand years, and when I wake, a mighty spruce tree will have raised me up high, high into the sky.

A nd now it is morning.

I crawl from the tent, wrapped in my grey blanket and look upward into the tree-tops. There are the sounds of birds – Swifts? Marbled Murrelets? I see that the sky is now clear and blue.

I eat a few Ritz crackers and another chocolate bar and my mouth desperately craves water. Still huddled inside the blanket and my business suit, I walk over the soft moss, down to the shore of the stream that flows below my tent. Clear water flows over a gravel bar; alders form a colony beside a deep pool in which schools of oolichan flutter like moods.

I kneel down and sip water from the pool. I raise my head and look through the clearing in the trees. I see the sun shining in the sky – a spinning ball of fire, like a burning basketball atop a finger. This is the same sun – the same burning orb of flame that shone over my youth – over swimming pools and Lego and Kraft dinner and malls and suburbia and TV and books about Andy Warhol. And this is the ball of fire that now shines on Mark, that burns his skin, that triggers cancer. This is the fire that shines on Stacey, that overheats her and makes her crave a drink. This is the fire that shines over Dana, the fire that will one day rain a destruction into his universe. And this is also the fire that shines on to Julie's house that makes her children play underneath the sprinkler. This is also the fire that feeds the trees that Todd plants. And this is also the sun that Kristy with her fair skin avoids, so that she can stay pretty and meet the man she will love forever.

I stare into this spinning ball of fire – the fire that burns and heats the winter – with no fear of blindness. I remove my blanket and fold it and place it on the warm rocks beside the water. I then remove my shoes and socks and stick my feet into the water, and oh, it is *so* cold.

I peel my clothes and step into the pool beside the burbling stream, on to polished rocks, and water so clear that it seems it might not even be really there.

My skin is grey, from lack of sun, from lack of bathing. And yes, the water is so cold, this water that only yesterday was locked as ice up on the mountaintops. But the pain from the cold is a pain that does not matter to me. I strip my pants, my shirt, my tie, my underwear and they lie strewn on the gravel bar next to my blanket.

And the water from the stream above me roars.

Oh, does it roar! Like a voice that knows only one message, one truth – never-ending, like the clapping of hands and the cheers of the citizens upon the coronation of the king, the crowds of the inauguration, cheering for hope and for that one voice that will speak to them.

Now – here is my secret:
    I tell it to you with an openness of heart that I
doubt I shall ever achieve again, so I pray that you are
in a quiet room as you hear these words. My secret is
that I need God – that I am sick and can no longer
make it alone. I need God to help me give, because I no
longer seem to be capable of giving; to help me be kind,
as I no longer seem capable of kindness; to help me
love, as I seem beyond being able to love.

I walk deeper and deeper into the rushing water. My testicles pull up into myself. The water enters my belly button and it freezes my chest, my arms, my neck. It reaches my mouth, my nose, my ears and the roar is so loud – this roar, this clapping of hands.

These hands – the hands that heal; the hands that hold; the hands we desire because they are better than desire.

I submerge myself in the pool completely. I grab my knees and I forget gravity and I float within the pool and yet, even here, I hear the roar of water, the roar of clapping hands.

These hands – the hands that care, the hands that mold; the hands that touch the lips, the lips that speak the words – the words that tell us we are whole.

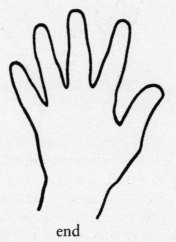

end

POSTSCRIPT

Life After God is, in many respects, life after *Generation X*. It is an alarming and enchanting meditation on the meaning of life and the nature of human relationships, which depicts a heartache hinted at but not previously explored in Coupland's other works. Set in and around Coupland's home town of Vancouver, and on the highways of North America, the book is made up of five melancholic tales filtered through the abstract, stilted, and surreal landscape of the mind.

As Coupland explains:

Vancouver is where my memory begins. It's the last city to be built, the last city on the edge of anything. All your dreams happen there. I went to a small school in a remote suburb next to a forest, beyond which there was nothing but more forest and tundra and the mountains and ice until the North Pole.

There is a sense that Coupland has returned to his roots to make sense of his life. He is working on a small canvas, in a microscopic world which he knows intimately. The tone, Coupland says, is due in part to the 'blizzard of personal losses – the deaths of friends and family'. Perhaps it is the alienation of personal loss, and the preoccupation with place and self, beginnings and incomplete endings, which informs the often haunting meanderings of *Life After God*.

Each story has a simple name, or theme of childlike credentials, such as 'Little Creatures', 'Things That Fly', and 'The Wrong Sun'. They also possess a profundity often associated with children's stories, such as *The Little Prince* and *Jonathan Livingstone Seagull*, which is enhanced by the naïve etchings which accompany them.

When *Life After God* was first published it confused the critics. Where was the acerbic cynicism, the irony, the lackadaisical rebellion of his previous tomes? Where was the classic Coupland, the pulse of the changing generations embroiled in consumerism?

Like the collapse of the Russian economy, where suddenly the rouble is worth nothing, in the case of

294

Coupland the postmodern irony has seemingly been displaced. Yet this is the problem of learning postmodernism by rote. It is not a new religion; it is the enunciation of a lack of all religion and as such marks a departure from the norms of narrative structure and accepted literary discourse.

In Coupland's writing everything is viewed through 3D specs: his characters are 'in the know'; they see another dimension. They recognize symbols and signifiers for lost generations and captured 'Elvis moments'. They observe icons in the twist of a scarf, the gait of a waitress, the muzac in the mall. What *Life After God* is perhaps suggesting is that these signifiers are not all. The signified is what counts: the emotion, the action, the event, the aftermath.

The search for meaning, though, is not in earnest, and is exposed as often being the product of most meaningless sequence of thought. In the story 'Patty Hearst', Brent says: 'You're always interpreting your dreams . . . why not interpret your everyday life as though it were a dream, instead'. By attributing this significance to events, rather than the more symbolic realm of dreams, the possibility of taking control of life whilst maintaining a relatively fresh approach to it becomes a possibility. Coupland seems to be suggesting that we are not awake to our lives, our selves. This, of course, is double-speak – the ability to wake up to yourself by viewing your life as you would your dreams is a subtlety typical of *Life After God*, marking a maturity in Coupland's writing about the emotionally dispossessed.

Anna Kiernan